Aunt Morbelia and the Screaming Skulls

Other Children's Books by Joan Carris

Just a Little Ham
Hedgehogs in the Closet
Rusty Timmons' First Million
Pets, Vets, and Marty Howard
Witch Cat
When the Boys Ran the House
The Revolt of 10-X
The Greatest Idea Ever

Aunt Morbelia and the Screaming Skulls

Joan Carris

Illustrated by Doug Cushman

LITTLE, BROWN AND COMPANY

Boston   Toronto   London

Text copyright © 1990 by Joan Davenport Carris
Illustrations copyright © 1990 by Doug Cushman

First edition

The characters and events in this book are fictitious. Any similarity to real
persons, living or dead, is coincidental and not intended by the author.

Library of Congress Cataloging-in-Publication Data

Carris, Joan Davenport.
    Aunt Morbelia and the screaming skulls/Joan Carris; illustrated
by Doug Cushman.
        p.   cm.
    Summary: The peaceful life of a boy with dyslexia is interrupted
when his great-aunt, who has a morbid fascination with ghosts and
death omens, moves in.
    ISBN 0-316-12945-3
    [1. Dyslexia — Fiction.   2. Great-aunts — Fiction.]   I. Cushman,
Doug, ill.   II. Title.
PZ7.C2347Au   1990
[Fic] — dc20   89-29241
                                                         CIP
                                                         AC

10 9 8 7 6 5 4

HC

Published simultaneously in Canada
by Little, Brown & Company (Canada) Limited

Printed in the United States of America

This book is dedicated to all the people, small and tall, who have struggled to overcome a learning disability in order to know the joys of reading.

Contents

Aunt Morbelia and the Screaming Skulls

1. The Terrible News

Todd Fearing left for Jeff's house right after dinner to tell him the terrible news.

"Wait a second," said his mother. "Take the Lorimers a plate of brownies."

Todd turned back. "Geez, Mom, we *never* have desserts. You just made those and now you're giving them all away."

Mrs. Fearing smiled and handed him the plate. "Too many sweets aren't good for us, remember? We still have some for tomorrow. Go on now, and don't drop the plate. And tell Anne Lorimer to call me about those draperies, okay? I have to order the fabric if she wants them finished in May."

"Okay." On the block-and-a-half walk to Jeff's house, Todd repeated, "Call about the draperies, call about the draperies." He had trouble remembering things, especially things that didn't matter, like draperies. He wasn't absentminded, just *different-minded*. Anyway, that's what they told him at the learning center.

Six Lorimers, all four kids and two parents, pounced on Todd and his brownies when he arrived.

"Call about the draperies, Mom said." There, he had remembered for once.

"Thanks, Todd," said Jeff's mother, giving him a swift hug. "I meant to call her today." She turned to the littlest Lorimer and removed a chubby hand from the brownie plate. "No more, Princess. Bedtime."

Princess was carried squalling out of the kitchen.

Jeff and Todd smiled as they watched her go. "She's spoiled something awful," Jeff said, shaking his head over his beloved baby sister.

Jeff's brothers — Jim, seventeen, and Duane, fourteen — said they had to study and left with brownies in hand.

"How about flashlight tag?" Jeff suggested.

"Later," Todd said. "Let's go outside, okay? I have to tell you something horribulous."

"You mean horrible," Jeff corrected on their way out. "It's h-o-r-r-i-b-l-e. Horrible."

"No, this time I think I got it right," Todd said as they sat down on the top porch step. "It's worse than horrible. It's horribulous."

"So what is it?"

"Great-Aunt Morbelia is coming to live with us."

Jeff began to grin. "I think this is another really good one," he said. His blond hair nearly stood on end in anticipation. "Nobody is named *Morbelia*, Todd. *Nobody.*"

"It is too Morbelia. I asked Dad to spell it and I wrote it down. See?"

Todd held out his napkin from dinner, a blue scrap with spaghetti sauce on it and three words: *Ophelia, Cordelia, Morbelia.*

Jeff stared at the words. "Unreal," he muttered. "Who has names like that?"

"My dad's aunts, that's who. Dad said Great-Aunt Ophelia was the oldest, then Cordelia, then their folks ran out of names from some old plays so they made up the last one — Morbelia. She's the one *we get.*" Todd rubbed his sneakers together in frustration before going on.

"Jeff, she's seventy-four! People that old are always at your dad's place — in boxes!"

"Caskets," Jeff said automatically. Jeff knew all about dead bodies and funerals. His father, James, was the fifth generation at Lorimer's Funeral Home in the small, historic town of Hampshire, Ohio.

Todd knew that Jeff admired James Lorimer — a large, blond, smiling man — and wanted to be like him. But Jeff planned to sit in a jet-pilot's seat, not work in a funeral home. Not even at Lorimer's, the finest funeral parlor in southern Ohio. Hampshire folk said that when Lorimer's was finished, a corpse looked positively happy to be dead.

Now Jeff said, "Seventy-four, huh? Heck, she could last a long time. Ladies are almost always older than men when they croak. Is she in a wheelchair or anything like that?"

"Mom said she's healthy as a horse, but she sounds weird."

"How weird? Like what?"

Todd thought about the last couple of days. Once he had entered their room and his parents had abruptly stopped talking. Tonight at dinner he had been sure they were not telling him everything. He didn't want his family to change. And this old lady would change things. He just knew it.

"Come on! I tell *you* everything, don't I?"

"Sure, sure," he replied, feeling good about their friendship, knowing it could never change. Nursery school, camp, and real school — they had always been together.

Jeff knew as much about Todd's learning problem, dyslexia, as Todd did. Jeff loved Todd's mix-ups with words. He repeated them fondly, as if they were jokes made on purpose. He knew Todd was a math and science whiz even if he couldn't spell *were* right every time. Or say the months in order. Surely next year, in seventh grade, thought Todd, I'll get those dumb months sorted out.

Refusing to dwell on words and the trouble they caused him, he tried to answer Jeff's question.

"Okay, first Dad said to Mom, 'She won't be here for a couple weeks, honey, so you'll have time to redo the guest room in solid black. She'll love that.' Then they laughed like crazy. What's funny about that?"

"Black? You're sure they said *black?*"

"Yup. Mom said Aunt Morbelia was a little strange."

"That's strange, all right. What else did they say?"

"They said I shouldn't pay any attention to what she said about owls and hellhounds and screaming gulls."

Jeff's fair face wrinkled with thought as he listened. "Owls, hellhounds, screaming gulls," he repeated.

"What's a hellhound anyway?" Todd asked.

"Who knows? Maybe a giant black dog like Inky."

"Nerd-brain." Todd socked Jeff in the arm. "Inky's a total wimp and you know it. But guess what else they said? They said Aunt Morbelia wouldn't like Banshee."

"Your cat?"

"My *black* cat, remember? Mom said Aunt Morbelia would think she was bad luck. And Banshee's the funniest pet we ever had! Dad promised I could keep her, though. He said Aunt Morbelia would just have to 'lighten up and join the real world' if she planned to live at our place."

Jeff shook his head. "Can't she go somewhere else?"

"Nope. Dad's sister and her husband live way out in California, and Aunt Morbelia won't go there. But she likes my dad, and Cordelia's dead now, so we get Morbelia."

"Can we still play pool at your place?"

"Sure! Mom said I should keep having guys over just like always. She said Aunt Morbelia would either like it or lump it. And if she lumps it, tough beanos, boy!"

"Yeah!" Jeff gave Todd a knowing look. "If she's a real pain, we can probably fix her, right?"

Todd grinned. He and Jeff had "fixed" several people over the years, often getting in trouble that way. Neither boy started fights, but they enjoyed finishing them.

Todd didn't want to talk anymore about his great-aunt Morbelia. He knew his life was going to change and he didn't want to think about it. "Come on, Jeff, let's get Alan and Rocky and the other guys for flashlight tag."

When Todd finally scooted in the back door, it was dark outside and his mom was waiting. "It's late," she said quietly, knowing he had trouble with time. Miss King, his teacher at the learning center, had explained that some dyslexic people easily lose track of time.

"Sorry, Mom. But can me and Jeff go fishing tomorrow after school?"

"I just know you mean *Jeff and I*," she said with a smile. "It's fine with me, as long as your room's picked up before you go to school. I have to show off your zippy plaid carpet tomorrow — and those built-in shelves."

"Aw, Mom, not again!" His mother's decorating clients drove Todd batty. They were forever traipsing through his house, oohing and aahing over its charm.

"That's the deal, Bud." She tipped her head to one side, considering him. "You know, Aunt Morbelia could take quite a shine to you. You look alike. Same big, dark eyes — tall, bony frame — and all that thick brown hair. Of course, her hair's white now."

Todd stared at her, aghast. He looked like an old lady? What a terrible thought!

She giggled then, giving herself away.

"Very funny," Todd said.

"Gotcha!"

"Hunh! Did not! Hey, Mom, let's read more of *The Sword in the Stone* now, okay? That's a really good one."

"Dad's reading tonight, Todd. I have to choose some samples for my client tomorrow. Go on, now. He's waiting."

Todd brushed his teeth quickly, eager to hear more about the young King Arthur. It was still so hard and so slow to read by himself. Just thinking about reading made him want to hit something — anything. Miss King promised he'd be reading well by high-school time. She'd been right about everything else and he trusted her, but he was sick of doing battle with the written word.

In bed, Todd folded his arms under his head and stared up at the ceiling while his dad read. He was imagining Wart, the boy-king, turned into a fish by the wizard Merlin. And Merlin, his white hair flying round his head. Ugh. Aunt Morbelia had white hair.

He sat up abruptly. "Dad, wait a minute. What was all that stuff at dinner about owls and hellhounds and screaming gulls? Remember?"

"Ah, those are just Aunt Morbelia's stories, Son." He looked off into space, remembering. "Poor old dear. She's obsessed with ghosts and death omens —

and I've never known a healthier woman. Or a more active one."

He looked at Todd. "But I said screaming *skulls*, Todd, not gulls."

Screaming skulls, Todd thought. Wait till I tell Jeff! He pictured a row of human skulls without flesh, their mouths wide open and shrieking. It was not a good picture at bedtime.

"Let's read some more, Dad, okay?"

2. *Aunt Morbelia Arrives*

In the two weeks before Aunt Morbelia's arrival, Todd asked his parents dozens of questions.

At length his dad said, "Look, Todd, I happen to love this old lady. She was extremely good to me as a boy. I know we haven't seen her in ages, but I still can't imagine packing her off to an old-folks' home. She'd be dead in two months from sheer depression."

"She sounds depressed anyway! What's the difference?"

"*We're* the difference," his mom said. "You, Dad, me, Inky, and Banshee. She needs a happy family experience and we're just the folks to provide it." His mother, known as "Sunny" instead of Sondra, gave one of her now-let's-be-cheerful smiles. She was hard to resist.

Todd gave up. He had seen the redecorated guest room — all sunlight and delicate green, with pure white blinds and white wicker furniture. Not a trace of black anywhere. A room of warmth with the promise of springtime.

"She's coming tomorrow," he told Inky one night in mid-April. Todd was sitting on his bed, Inky on the floor, his broad black head resting in Todd's lap. With all of his faithful Labrador heart, Inky loved Todd. His doggy hind end squirmed in delight on the rug as Todd talked to him.

Banshee padded into the room and leapt to the bed. "Meoww," she said, settling herself, deliberately placing her nose in front of Inky's where it rested on Todd's leg.

Inky shifted his head to Todd's other leg. "Hrrr," he warned, eyes on Banshee.

Banshee twitched her whiskers and sl-ow-ly lowered her eyelids, peering at Inky through sea green slits.

"You guys just cool it," Todd said. "Aunt Morbelia's coming and we all have to be nice, got it?"

Inky whimpered agreeably.

"I'm not worried about you. It's this Banshee cat," Todd said, stroking the black satin body. "She's bad."

Banshee was bad. In her four years she had done all the things Inky had never thought of — even to chewing socks. Day after day, patient, gentlemanly Inky tried to teach her some manners. Unlike Banshee, he thought slowly and dimly.

Everyone except Inky realized that this cat wouldn't be taught. Banshee was Banshee — saved only by her shimmering grace and melodious purr. She was purring now, filling Todd's room with the richness of her sound.

Trying to think positively like his mom, Todd remembered she had said his great-aunt loved to bake. Well, that was one good thing anyway.

Just before dinner the next evening, the Fearings heard a car door slam outside. "She's here," said Mr. Fearing, leaping to his feet. "Come on, Sunny, Todd."

Todd stood beside his mom on the front stoop and watched his father help Aunt Morbelia out of the car. A neighbor of hers in Philadelphia had driven her down to Hampshire.

The neighbor, an elderly man, began lifting suitcases out of the backseat.

"Let me do that," protested Mr. Fearing.

Mrs. Fearing ran to hug Aunt Morbelia and help with the suitcases. Todd couldn't take his eyes off his great-aunt. He felt glued to the brick stoop.

No one had said she was so tall. And straight. Her black skirt nearly swept the ground. Atop a mass of the whitest hair sat a black hat with a black veil.

She lifted the veil and stared at him. Her dark eyes burned into him. Seeing right through me, he thought.

She knows I don't want her. She knows. And she doesn't want to be here. I can feel it.

"Inky," Todd called. "Here, Inky."

Inky nosed open the screen door and joined Todd on the stoop. "Rroof," he said cheerfully, tail wagging. Inky loved company.

Aunt Morbelia stepped back a pace and pointed a

bony finger at Inky. "You did not warn me!" she said, making the sign of the cross with her other hand.

Mr. Fearing's gaze followed the accusing finger. "Oh, that's our Inky — a pussycat, really." He laughed briefly. "More so than our cat, who's a terror. Hey, Todd, give us a hand. The trunk's loaded, too."

Todd gripped Inky's collar and forced his feet down the steps. Come on, he told himself. You're being a baby. This is a little old lady, for crum's sake.

Except that she wasn't little. She was as tall as his father, six feet anyway — all of it solid black. And she had powerful eyes. He had never felt eyes like hers.

"This is Todd," said his dad as he approached the car. "He's in sixth grade now, and if you have a problem with math, he's your man."

Her hand shot out and gripped Todd's chin, lifting his face so that he had to look at her. Under amazingly dark eyebrows, her eyes were an unusual, charcoal gray, with paler gray smudges beneath. She had a big, straight nose like his dad, and the same wide mouth.

"Well, he is yours, all right," Aunt Morbelia said to Mr. Fearing, all the while gripping Todd's chin.

"Of course I'm his," Todd croaked, amazed he could even talk. He had an odd feeling in his stomach, too. "Who else would I be?"

His mom moved closer. "She meant that the Fearings have a strong resemblance to one another, Todd, that's all."

"Yes," Aunt Morbelia said, releasing her hold on Todd's chin, letting her hand drop to her side.

She went on, her voice cool and precise. "I shall try not to interfere in your life, Todd. I am sure that your parents did not consult you about my moving in." She smiled then, but it was a bitter token.

Inky nudged Aunt Morbelia's hand with his head. Visitors always petted him, and this one hadn't.

This time the visitor snatched her hand away.

"He just wants you to pet him," said Todd. "He likes people. And . . . and they did, too, ask me about you moving in. . . . And I said fine." He wasn't sure why he had to say that, but he did.

Again he felt the power of her eyes. In a low voice she said, "You have a good heart, Todd, but you are a bad liar."

"It's getting awfully chilly out here," Mrs. Fearing said. "Let's hurry, Todd, and unload the trunk." She grabbed his hand and pulled him toward the back of the car.

"Geez, Mom," Todd whispered, "she already decided I hate her, she called me a liar, and she *never petted Inky!*"

"Honey, I'm so *proud of you*," his mom whispered back. "Here, take this box of books. It weighs a ton."

His head in the trunk next to his mother's, Todd hissed, "Mom, this isn't going to work!"

His mom giggled. "It may be trickier than we thought. But it's three against one. No, four, counting Inky." She pinched his cheek. "Come on, kid, where's your fighting spirit?"

Hah! he thought. Fighting spirit, phooey! He

lugged the heavy box toward the house while his mother carried a clothes bag. "She'll probably put Banshee in a pie," he muttered.

"I've thought of that myself sometimes," said his mom.

Finally, the suitcases, clothes bags, and heavy boxes were in the house, most of them upstairs in the redecorated room. Aunt Morbelia carried in the final items herself — two enormous, framed pictures of her ancestors. They all wore black. All had big noses and wide mouths and dark hair. Fearings every one.

She propped the ancient Fearings on the bottom step to get a better hold just as Banshee peered down the stairs. Banshee hated company. She streaked down the staircase, flew past Aunt Morbelia, and out the front door.

"Aah!" shrieked Aunt Morbelia, dropping her ancestors. She stumbled over to a chair and collapsed into it like folded cardboard. "I must leave immediately."

Mr. Fearing hurried over to her. "Now, Aunt —"

"Bruce, save your breath. When a black cat crosses my path, it is an evil omen. You know that as well as I do. I was a fool to let you talk me into this."

"That's crazy," Todd said without stopping to think. "Banshee's our pet. She runs in front of us all the time. It doesn't mean a thing!"

"Her name is *Banshee*?" asked Aunt Morbelia, white-faced. "And she *lives* here? With that — that

black hellhound?" Again she pointed at Inky, who sat nearby, still waiting for the visitor to pet him.

Inky panted hopefully. When someone pointed at him, he was usually taken for a walk — or fed dinner.

The elderly neighbor from Philadelphia spoke up. "Now, Morbelia," he began soothingly.

"Don't 'Now-Morbelia' me! I have never seen so many bad omens in such a short time. All telling me I am making a ghastly mistake." She rose to her feet. "We can load that car up right now and drive back to Philadelphia."

Todd was fascinated. Inky a hellhound? Banshee a bad omen? He didn't dare look at his mother. If their eyes met, it'd be all over. Once they'd gotten the giggles so badly in church that they'd had to leave.

Mrs. Fearing said, "We can talk about this over dinner, but nobody's going anywhere until we've eaten my veal stroganoff." She pointed at the dog. "Give Inky a quick walk, Todd, and then we'll eat."

"Rrooof!" yelped Inky, eyes on her finger. Now he knew something good was going to happen.

Over dinner, Mr. Fearing spoke about the joys of owning a Labrador retriever. Mr. Mason agreed, describing the Lab he'd had as a boy.

"And besides," Mr. Fearing went on, "only a gentleman like Inky would put up with our cat."

He leaned toward Aunt Morbelia. "Really, dear, Banshee has kept us laughing for four years. You should have seen Sunny's face the day we found her asleep in the dryer."

On hearing Banshee's name, Aunt Morbelia looked around nervously, her fork clattering against her plate.

"She's outside for the night," Todd said.

Aunt Morbelia put down her fork and spoke to Todd's father. "I see what you are trying to do, Bruce, and I am not ungrateful. You were a warm-hearted, generous boy, and you have not changed. But I have. I am old now — an old spinster in mourning for her dead sister. I live in one world, you live in another."

She shook her head. "No, my dear, it simply is not going to work."

Todd couldn't watch her face any longer. He stared down at his plate and felt awful. Boy, he thought, what a mess.

His mother leaned across the table. "I am going to be insulted if you leave before giving us a chance," she announced.

Aunt Morbelia sat up straighter.

"And terribly disappointed," Mrs. Fearing went on. "I had counted on your teaching me to bake bread and rolls — and your help with Todd's lessons — and your room is absolutely yummy and it was just going to waste up there —"

"Todd's lessons?" Aunt Morbelia interrupted. "What do you mean? Is he not enrolled in school?"

Mr. Fearing explained about dyslexia and how

Todd went to a learning center that gave him special homework.

"I'm sure my dad, your brother, was dyslexic," Mr. Fearing told his aunt. "He was brilliant — we all knew that — but he never mastered reading or spelling, and that's not logical. They say dyslexia is inherited, of course. It missed me, but it zapped our Todd."

"Yeah, lucky me," Todd said, filled with old, familiar anger.

"What exactly is it?" persisted Aunt Morbelia.

"A learning disorder," Todd replied curtly.

"We can explain all that tomorrow," said Mrs. Fearing, jumping to her feet. "It's not all bad — Todd's brighter than anyone in the house — he just learns in a different way. But we shouldn't bore Mr. Mason with all this."

She turned to Aunt Morbelia's neighbor. "You'll want to be on the road for Cincinnati soon, won't you? I understand you're going to visit your son's family."

Mr. Mason looked at his watch. "Yes, but it's only an hour's drive," he said. "Morbelia, you ought to try this out for a while. We've been neighbors over thirty years, known each other a long time, and this is the only chance you've had. Understand me?"

"Yes, Thomas, you needn't lecture." Aunt Morbelia stood up and began clearing the table.

Todd watched her face and saw that she was just as worried as he was. But she's going to try it, he thought. Because of *me*. Oh, brother.

Mrs. Fearing served coffee and cookies.

"Store-bought cookies," chided Aunt Morbelia, with a small smile for Todd's mother. The smile vanished as she turned to Mr. Fearing.

"Tell me why you named that cat Banshee," she demanded.

"She's got a terrible yowl," said Todd's dad. "If she's upset, the world knows it, so I named her Banshee. Probably because I've never forgotten your stories."

He reached across the table to squeeze his aunt's hand. "You're the best storyteller I know."

"They are not just stories," Aunt Morbelia said. "When I hear the banshee wail, I know what it means."

Oh yeah? Todd wondered. Still, the strange look on his aunt's face made his stomach feel funny. A banshee sounded creepy. He hated stuff like that.

3. The Wail of the Banshee

Around eight, Aunt Morbelia's neighbor left and the adults began cleaning up the kitchen. Todd went upstairs to his parents' room to phone Jeff.

"Sounds pretty heavy, all right," Jeff said after he heard what Todd had to say. "What's a banshee anyhow?"

"You got me."

"How about if I come over and we ask her?"

No way, Todd thought. Jeff hadn't seen his great-aunt, so he had no idea of what they were up against. To Jeff he said, "Sorry. Dad said no promotion tonight because Aunt Morbelia's tired from her trip."

Jeff began to chuckle — loudly — right in Todd's ear.

"Okay, okay!" He had done it again.

"Sorry, but it's a kinda good one. Not one of your best, but good. See, I'm pretty sure your dad said 'No *commotion*.' C-o-m-m-o-t-i-o-n. Lots of noise and people."

As soon as he heard the word, especially with Jeff's

hearty emphasis, he knew his mistake. Just a few dumb letters, for crum's sake! Why can't I remember a few —

"Hey, Todd, you there?"

"Yeah."

"Look, it's okay, you know that! I help you with words, you help me with math. That's fair, isn't it?"

Todd answered slowly. "I guess so."

"You sure I can't come over?" Jeff pleaded.

"I'm sure. But tomorrow you could."

"Ask her about the banshee, okay?"

Todd remembered his great-aunt's face when she had talked about the banshee. And again, a cold, creepy feeling came over him. Then he asked himself, Am I a wimp or what?

To Jeff he said, "Sure. Sure, I'll ask her. Bye."

He went to his room, more than ready to hear another chapter of *The Sword in the Stone*. When it was over he said, "Mom, I have to ask Aunt Morbelia something. Is she asleep?"

"I doubt it. I helped her hang those pictures of old, dead Fearings just before we started reading." She shook her head. "They have completely ruined my lovely effect. Instant gloom. I can't believe it."

"I can. Remember who said this might be tricky?"

"Wise guy," she teased. "You aren't going to ask for one of her stories, are you? Because you have the world's best imagination, Bud, and —"

"I know, I know," he said, leaping out of bed. "But I'm not a wimp, okay?"

She shrugged. "Fine. Just don't tell *me*. Ghost stories give me the willies."

Todd found his great-aunt wearing a navy robe, her white hair in a thick braid. She was reading in the new wicker rocker. Her door was ajar, and he saw her before she saw him.

Now . . . now she looked old. Before, strong willed and stiffly upright, she hadn't seemed old. Or sad.

She isn't really reading, he thought, just pretending. Like I do sometimes. He sighed. Poop on Jeff, anyway. I always get talked into —

"Good evening, Todd." Even her voice sounded older.

"Uh . . . hi!" he said, wishing he'd had the sense to stay in bed. "How's the room?"

"Lovely. Your mother has the gift of beauty — in many ways. But you did not come to talk about my room."

"Well, no, not exactly," he replied, edging onto the pale lemon carpet. "I was wondering . . . well . . . about the banshee. I didn't know our cat had a bad name."

"Your father did not tell you?"

"No."

"Sit down, please." She motioned him to the bed. She folded her hands in her lap and gazed off into space, a dark look into nothing. Then she spoke.

"The banshee comes for all of us sooner or later. She is a spirit from the other world who tells us when our life is over. I have heard her wailing cry many times. Wailing for people I loved. And she took them every time."

Todd chewed on his lip. "Did . . . did you ever see her?"

"Yes, long ago, when I was a girl. I went outdoors at night when I heard her call my father's name. She was moaning his name, over and over, and then I saw her — in her white grave clothes, her pale hair streaming out behind her as she floated across the garden — coming closer and closer.

"I saw the bones through the grayed flesh of her outstretched hands. Black holes where there should have been eyes. . . .

"I think I screamed, and she drifted away in the mist, still wailing. In the morning, my father was dead."

Geez! Todd thought, eyes riveted on his great-aunt. She had given the banshee a terrible reality. He whispered, "Can't . . . can't you just tell her to go away?"

"The banshee goes where she wants."

"Well she doesn't come around *here*. Reverend Parker wouldn't let her."

Aunt Morbelia shifted in her chair. "And who is he, may I ask?"

"He's our minister at First Presbyterian. And he's never said anything about a banshee."

"An American, I expect," she said. "I grew up in England, Todd. I know many things that Americans do not."

His mind spun, hurling a zillion questions to the surface. "So is a banshee an English ghost?"

"She is from Ireland, and she only appears to certain families. *Like ours*," she added.

Todd had no wish to argue, certainly not now. I'll ask Dad, he decided, yawning. It had been an oddly tiring day.

"Cover your mouth!"

Todd slapped a hand over his mouth. "Why?" he asked, voice muffled.

"Because the Devil can get in through your mouth when you yawn," she replied. "I thought everyone knew that."

Todd kept his hand in place. "He can?"

"Yes. Also, it is polite to cover a yawn."

"Is the Devil gone now? Can I move my hand?"

Her lips curved slightly. "Yes, and we should go to bed. But tell me what you like for breakfast. Cinnamon rolls or caramel rolls?"

Todd nearly drooled on the new flowered spread. "Hot sweet rolls?" he asked, unbelieving.

"I always bake early in the morning."

"Yahoo!" he yelled, vaulting off the bed. "Sorry," he said, seeing her flinch. "See, Mom never makes that stuff. I don't think she knows how. I don't care what kind they are, but can I take one to Jeff?"

"Who is Jeff?"

"My friend. He's real nice. You'll like him."

Aunt Morbelia stood up, tall and straight again. "I am sure I shall if you do. Of course you can share the rolls. And thank you for visiting me on my first night here. That was very thoughtful."

"Oh . . . no problem. I mean . . . good," he said, escaping into the hall.

Back in his room, Todd dove into bed and felt for Inky with his feet. Inky would scare away any banshee, just in case it came in the night. Just in case it wanted to visit any more members of the Fearing family.

Inky wriggled north until he was stretched full-length against Todd, on top of the blanket. He gave one tiny whimper of pleasure and went back to snoring.

I sure hope Banshee doesn't yowl, Todd thought, dreading the sound that had often wakened his family. If she does that tonight, Aunt Morbelia will probably croak.

Unbidden, the image of the eyeless, wailing banshee floated into his mind. Jeff would ask all about her. He must remember. Todd had a horrible feeling that the banshee would be easy to remember.

The next morning, Todd and his father were each savoring a third caramel roll when Jeff knocked and bounced in through the kitchen door.

"Wow! What smells so good?" he asked, eyes on the tall black figure at the sink.

Startled, Aunt Morbelia jerked her arm across the counter, sending salt, baking powder, and brown sugar to the floor.

"Aaah," she cried, eyes on the floor. She bent down, took a pinch of something white, and threw it back over her left shoulder.

Jeff retreated to the door.

"Salt?" asked Mr. Fearing.

"An ominous way to begin the day," Aunt Morbelia said bleakly. "Bruce, isn't it obvious —"

"No, dear, it's not," he replied, getting up from his chair. He took a dustpan and brush from the cupboard and began sweeping up the mess.

"What's obvious," he continued, "is that you're not used to boys, so it will take some time." He rose, handed her the dustpan, and kissed her on the cheek.

"Those were the best rolls I've eaten since the last time I had your rolls. Now explain to the boys — this is Jeff Lorimer, by the way — about the salt, because I have to be downtown in ten minutes. See you tonight."

"Yeah, tell us about the salt," Todd said.

"It's bad luck," said Jeff, his hand on the doorknob. "My gramma told me."

"Salt is bad luck?" asked Todd.

"Just spilling it." Aunt Morbelia frowned. "Also it is clumsy and it always makes me mad. When you spill it, you must throw some over your left shoulder, where the Devil lurks. That chases him away."

"Oh yeah?" Jeff said, his eyes on the plate of rolls.

"Here," Todd said, holding up the plate.

Jeff came slowly toward the table, where desire won out. He took a roll in each hand. After only one bite, he looked at Todd's great-aunt and said, "Do you do this a lot?"

Todd saw her mouth twitch, but she didn't laugh. *I don't think she knows how*, he decided.

"I bake something most days," she admitted. "The way you boys eat, I guess I had better." She leaned toward Jeff, her eyes on his face. "Hmm. You should make a wish."

Jeff drew back nervously. "Why?"

"You have an eyelash on your cheek."

"So I get to make a wish?"

"Yes, and if you guess which cheek the eyelash is on, your wish will come true."

"Hey, that's cool! I wish —"

"Don't tell," Todd interrupted, looking at his aunt. "You're not supposed to tell, right?"

She nodded. "That is correct, Todd."

"Okay," Jeff said. "I wished. And I'm guessing the eyelash's on my right cheek."

"Bingo! Slap me five!" Todd cheered.

Aunt Morbelia watched them slap each other's hands. "Slap me five," she repeated. "How interesting."

Jeff gave her a long look, then asked, "Can I have another roll?"

Todd's mother dashed into the kitchen. "Did it again," she said breathlessly. "Boy, am I a champion sleeper. Morbelia, what are you doing up? I don't expect you to make breakfast every day, for heaven's sake."

She turned to the boys. "You kids better hit the road. It's late."

Todd and Jeff grabbed their books and began jogging toward school. "Well, what do you think?" Todd asked.

"Ran beeya?" Jeff queried, mouth full of caramel roll.

Todd translated that as "your aunt Morbelia."

"Yeah, what do you think?"

Jeff swallowed. "Great cook! But, man, she's strange. Tell me about the banshee."

Todd repeated Aunt Morbelia's words — every one. "And I had a creepy dream about it, too." He didn't say just how creepy, or how great it had been to have Inky there when he woke up, terrified from the nightmare. More than anything else, he hated nightmares and horror stories.

"She knows weird stuff," Jeff commented, "but she doesn't know all the regular stuff, like 'slap me five.' I guess she hasn't been around kids, huh?"

"Just ghosts, I think."

4. Strange Days

Within a week of his great-aunt's arrival, Todd knew dozens of things he hadn't known before. It was bad luck to spill salt, to yawn without covering your mouth, to count the stars, to comb your hair after dark, to see a crow, to hear a whippoorwill near the house. Even dreaming of cabbages was an ill omen. It was an endless list.

Todd's mother kept urging Aunt Morbelia to get out and see the town. "I want you to enjoy yourself," she insisted. But Aunt Morbelia worked in the house or the yard, quiet and grave in manner.

Aunt Morbelia shrank whenever she saw Banshee, and she ignored Inky. Still, Inky waited for her to pet him. When she sat down, he planted his rear end on the hem of her long skirt, just as a hint.

I have to talk to Dad, Todd decided one evening. Aunt Morbelia had snatched the parsley from everyone's dinner plate, saying it was an unlucky plant.

"I am amazed you brought that in the house," she said.

"Ignorance is bliss," replied Mrs. Fearing. She was wearing her now-let's-be-cheerful smile.

Dinner over, Todd said, "Dad, let's walk Inky, okay?"

"Sure thing." Mr. Fearing jumped up, grabbed Inky's leash, and they were out the door in seconds.

Todd didn't waste any time either. "She's totally wacko, Dad, and I don't like it. This isn't going to work!"

Inky stopped to examine a particularly interesting smell, so they all stopped.

Todd's dad said, "I knew that's what you were going to say. I admit she's worse than she was, but we can't give up yet. At least Banshee's staying out of the way."

"For now she is," Todd warned.

Inky pulled them forward. As they moved on down the street, Mr. Fearing continued. "I think that a large part of her gloominess is a reaction to being in a strange place. Also, she's sad about Cordelia's death. Her whole life has changed now — everything. That has to be tough."

Todd tried to understand because his dad wanted him to. Still, he could not imagine what it would be like to be in Aunt Morbelia's black shoes.

Mr. Fearing began to chuckle. "Remember what she said about the bats?"

Todd grinned. She had said, very seriously one evening as he was leaving for Jeff's house, "Be careful about bats. They are out at night, you know, and it is unlucky to have one land on your head."

"It sure is!" Todd had replied. They had all laughed then. Even Aunt Morbelia had smiled.

Now he and his dad laughed again, remembering. "I think," Mr. Fearing said, "that we all must remember what a difficult life she's had up till now.

"She was just over twenty when her parents died and she came to America with her sisters. Ophelia had a job as a nanny here. Morbelia finished her degree and taught school for more than thirty years before she had to nurse Ophelia, who died a slow, miserable death. Just recently, she nursed Cordelia and watched her die."

"I know, and she heard the banshee wail each time."

"Well, she *thinks* she did, and what people believe shapes their lives."

"But she saw the banshee! She told me."

Mr. Fearing shook his head. "Son, she was sick with a fever. The whole family was sick. Yorkshire had a deadly influenza that year — the kind that often led to pneumonia. Her father died of it and her mother a few months later. I think it weakened Ophelia and Cordelia, too. Morbelia was always the healthiest of the lot."

"Yeah! She was scrubbing the kitchen floor today when I got home from school. Mom came in and just had a fit. She made her quit and have tea and cookies."

"Good for Mom," said Mr. Fearing. "But, Todd, think about it. Here's Aunt Morbelia — up at dawn, forecasting Doom every second — but *meanwhile* she bakes a few dozen rolls, a loaf of bread, weeds the garden, scrubs the floor. . . ."

He grinned broadly. "The Grim Reaper will have a long wait for her, if you ask me."

"You mean Death?"

"Well, you learned that fast. Don't let her talk get you down, okay? We have to show her that life can be fun."

Oh sure, Todd thought as he turned Inky around. She can't even laugh. Out loud he said, "Come on, Dad, we have to go back. I got tons of work from Miss King today."

"Why not ask Aunt Morbelia to help?"

"Do I have to?"

"No, but she's a born teacher. The best I know."

"She doesn't know about dyslexic kids!"

His dad looked at his watch. "Right now, at seven P.M. on Tuesday night, no. By next week, she will. Trust me."

Todd kept quiet. If *you* had dyslexia, he thought, you wouldn't want everybody thinking about it. Too many people know already, for crum's sake.

"Trust me, Todd. Come on, let's jog. I'll bet I've put on five pounds since the Mad Baker moved in."

When Todd got out his homework, he still didn't want to ask his aunt for help. She was sitting under the floor lamp in the living room, darning a sock.

Ever hopeful, Inky sat beside her, pinning her skirt to the floor and waiting.

Todd eyed his dog and thought, What if I sat there too? I don't want help, but I really hate doing homework alone. Before he chickened out he plopped himself on the floor next to Inky. "Okay if I share your light?" he asked.

"Certainly." She leaned forward and watched him open his notebook. "Your mother has been trying to answer my questions about dyslexia. I believe that some of my students must have had your problem. That bothers me."

Oh boy, Todd thought. Why don't we just fly a banner from the roof that says: NOTICE! DYSLEXIC KID INSIDE! Still, his aunt obviously cared, and so he tried to explain.

"Miss King says we're all different, every one of us. I have trouble remembering things — mainly words. I mix them up. And I forget what time it is. Even the day sometimes," he added bitterly.

She peered down at his workbook. One row of words read, *Beat, neat, seat, peat, heat, meat, repeat.*

"I see. And the months? Your mother said that it was hard for you to say them in order."

Unconsciously, Todd clenched his fists. Not knowing the months made him furious. "I'll figure it out," he said.

"Just learn the cold months first. January, February, March. That's all. Forget the others for now."

He had never thought of it that way. The cold months. January, February, March. January, February, March. He could do it already. Of course, by tomorrow morning . . .

Before he forgot, Todd wrote *January, Febuary, March* at the top of his notebook.

"Good," she said. "Now close your eyes and see them and say them. Imagine them on the paper — only we shall put another *r* in February. *Feb-ru-ary*." She wrote while he watched.

Todd wrote *February* five times. Miss King loved to see him do that. Sometimes he wrote words in fingerpaint or in sand, over and over. Even though it seemed dopey, it was the answer. He knew that now.

The homework time sped by. When they finished Aunt Morbelia said, "I admire your determination, Todd. I can see that is what it takes. Now, will you do me a favor?"

"I'll try," he said uneasily.

"Bring your friends home tomorrow. Your mother says that you often have friends in. I do not want you to stop because of me."

"Well . . . we're kind of noisy."

"Yes, but I used to like the sounds of boys having fun. And this is your house, after all."

Todd knew he should say, "It's your house, too," but it wasn't her house. Not yet. Maybe never. She was only trying it out as Mr. Mason had suggested. And so he said, "Kids like to come here because we have a pool table. We have tournaments all the time."

"I understand. Just remember, you will be doing me a favor by being yourself. I do not want to interfere."

Easy favor, he thought. He wondered if he might ask something of her.

"Aunt Morbelia," he said, hesitating a bit, "could you just pet Inky once? He's been waiting a week now and he can't understand why you won't pet him."

"Do you think it is bothering him?"

"I know it is."

"Then will he stop perching on my skirt when I sit?"

Todd smiled. "Maybe."

She reached out slightly and Inky leaned forward to meet her hand. He whimpered as her long, strong fingers touched him. His eyes closed in ecstasy.

"He feels rather like an old horsehair sofa," she said. "I have always been afraid of dogs, especially black ones. A big one bit Cordelia and I have never forgotten." She tapped Inky's head daintily while she talked, as if teaching herself to pet a dog.

Moving half an inch at a time, Inky shifted his hind end until he sat in front of Aunt Morbelia. He laid his head in her lap, sighed with pleasure, and looked up at her face.

"He likes me," she said, amazed.

"Sure he does. Well, Mom's waiting to read, okay? If you get sick of Inky, just say 'Down.'"

Rigid in her chair, Aunt Morbelia nodded.

Todd bounded up the steps, then turned and peeked around the corner. Inky would come up soon, Todd knew, but for now he had Aunt Morbelia right where he wanted her.

5. Aunt Morbelia's Story

You'd better warn 'em," Jeff told Todd as they stood by their lockers the next afternoon. "I mean, when they first see her — bam! you know? She's not just any old lady."

"Right," Todd agreed. "Here they come. Hey, Alan, Rocky, over here!"

Alan Harriman shifted his pile of books and headed toward them. He had wavy, light brown hair and thick eyeglasses. Once he had told Todd, "When I lose my glasses I can't find my way out of my closet." He was the smartest person Todd knew.

Rocky was the prettiest and the toughest. No one had dared to call her RosaLynn in years. She wore ancient docksiders, jeans, and T-shirts, and kept her spun-gold hair cut short, but nothing helped. She was still pretty, still a girl. And lately, Todd thought she'd been different somehow. He couldn't say exactly how, just different.

As the four pushed open the school door, Todd said, "I have to tell you guys something. My Aunt

Morbelia lives at our house now. She's sort of weird, but she likes kids."

"And she cooks great," added Jeff. "Hey," he said, looking up, "it's going to pour any minute. Let's run."

"How's come she lives with you?" Rocky asked, jogging along beside Todd.

"What do you mean, weird?" asked Alan.

Todd needed all of the two-block trot to his house to explain his great-aunt.

"She sounds cool," Rocky said. "Maybe she'll tell us a scary story. I love that stuff! My Aunt Sarah just blabs about her perfect kids all the time. Makes me puke."

Todd thought, scary story, barf. I hope Aunt Morbelia stays in her room.

But she was waiting for them, looming tall and black in the doorway to Todd's house.

Rocky caught her breath and ducked behind Jeff. It was the first timid thing Todd had ever seen her do.

"Sheesh," Alan whispered, clutching his books.

"Welcome," said Aunt Morbelia, sweeping aside her skirts and flinging open the door.

Todd went in first, followed by Jeff, then Alan, head down. Last, a silent Rocky, who stared straight ahead.

Oh great, thought Todd. I might as well have a live-in Dracula.

But few things frightened Jeff, who had grown up in the funeral business. He smiled up at Todd's

aunt and said, "I don't suppose you baked anything more?"

"How kind of you to remember," she replied. "As it happens, I baked bread today."

"All right!" Jeff grinned at her as if they'd been best buddies since kindergarten. "I thought I smelled something good in here."

Two slabs of warm bread later, her mouth rimmed with butter and brown sugar, Rocky finally talked. "Can you show my mom how to make this? It's even better than pizza."

"Why don't I show you?" offered Aunt Morbelia. "I was baking rolls and bread when I was your age."

Rocky looked down at her plate. "No thanks. Girls cook. I don't."

"I see," Aunt Morbelia said. "And what do *you* do?"

Alan spoke first. "She runs faster than anybody in our class, she beats us at pool, and she punches us out if we call her RosaLynn." His large, near-sighted eyes got even larger as he realized what he'd said.

"Sleazebag! Just wait, boy."

"Aw, come on, Rocky," Todd said. "Nobody's called you that all year. Give us a break."

Aunt Morbelia leaned forward, her penetrating eyes on Rocky. "You do have a lovely name. The Tudor rose is the badge of England. . . . And roses speak of love. Of course, you do not want them to bloom in the fall, and sometimes they cause ship-wreck, but probably not in southern Ohio."

"You hear that? I can cause shipwrecks." Rocky beamed. "But why shouldn't roses bloom in the fall?"

"Because then diseases follow through the winter. Roses are not meant to bloom in autumn."

"That's not logical," said Alan.

Quickly Todd asked, "How about some pool?" He knew Alan was all set to demand what he called "hard, cold facts" about fall-blooming roses.

"Yeah, let's get going," urged Jeff. "We've got a funeral at seven so I have to be home early for dinner."

"Funeral?" Aunt Morbelia asked faintly. "You poor child. Was it someone close to you?"

Todd opened his mouth to explain, but Jeff didn't give him a chance. "No, just some old guy from a town near here," he told Aunt Morbelia. "He was all yellow, too. Dad said his liver was a wreck. He had trouble making him look good, but now I think he looks great. That's why we got him, of course. Nobody else could have pulled it off."

"Merciful heavens," murmured Aunt Morbelia, one hand at her throat.

"Not to worry," Todd told her. "Jeff's dad is an undertaker. Lorimer's Funeral Home. It's a nice place."

"You bet," said Alan. "My grampa wouldn't think of going anywhere else."

"We'll take you on a tour sometime," Jeff promised Aunt Morbelia. "You'll like it. We play great music — happy orchestra stuff, you know? Dad says going home to God is a beautiful thing, so that's how we do it."

Aunt Morbelia was speechless.

"Where's Mom?" Todd asked, afraid his great-aunt would faint or have a heart attack. She looked queer. "And where's Inky?"

Aunt Morbelia rose unsteadily from her chair. "Your mother has a client in her office. Inky is there, too," she said, her voice gradually gaining strength.

"And that ill-omened fiend is on my bed, Todd. I want her out of my room before I go in there. I meant to say that straightaway when you came home, only I was so glad to see you had missed the storm that I forgot." Just then, thunder grumbled nearby.

"Come on, you guys!" Jeff said again.

"No, wait," Rocky commanded, turning to Todd. "What's an ill-omened fiend? I want to see it."

"Just Banshee," Todd said. "A black cat's bad luck, remember? Now let's go."

Rocky shook her head. "We can play pool anytime," she said, whirling around to face Todd's aunt. "You know such great stuff! Could you tell us a really creepy story? Those *Friday the Thirteenth* movies are my all-time favorites. I love being scared like that!"

Oh no, thought Todd. He always felt like such a wimp when she said how much she enjoyed being scared. He hadn't seen any of those movies. He thought they sounded sick — not one bit funny or entertaining.

"Todd's father used to love learning about ghosts," Aunt Morbelia said, as the thunder came closer. She sat back down at the table. "Of course, ghosts in England are common. People see them all the time, especially in the Tower of London and at Hampton Court. In the old stone manor houses, too. Ghosts have an affinity for stone, you see."

BOOOM! Lightning cracked as the storm moved in. The kitchen grew dim and raindrops sounded on the porch roof outside the kitchen windows.

"Perfect timing," Alan whispered to Todd.

"Yeah," breathed Jeff. "Just like a movie."

Todd tried to smile. I am obviously not normal, he thought. My folks got a dud. Everybody else loves being scared stiff. I like those old Abbott and Costello movies, and *Tom and Jerry* cartoons. *Yogi Bear . . .*

BOOOM! went the lightning again. The lights in the kitchen flickered and went out.

"Ooooh," shivered Rocky.

"Once there was a girl from Yorkshire, where I lived," began Aunt Morbelia. "Her name was Anne Griffith — a young gentlewoman who lived at Burton Agnes Hall during the reign of the first Queen Elizabeth. Anne loved the hall and told everyone she would never leave it.

"As she was lying on her deathbed she cried, 'Oh my sisters, keep me here always. When I am dead, remove my head and place it in the house. Promise me! Promise!' With her last breath she begged them, 'Do not bury my head!'

"Her sisters promised, thinking she was not in her right mind, but they buried her intact. They dressed her in her loveliest gown, put a wreath of flowers in

45

her hair, and closed the coffin, placing it in the family vault.

"Only days later, her parents and sisters woke at night to hear a ghoulish moaning and crying that filled the manor house. They sent servants and young men searching, but none could find the source of the piercing cries.

"Over and over, shrieks and dying moans echoed through the house. Night after night — until the family was ill for lack of sleep.

"At last Anne's sisters went to see their minister. He reminded them of their deathbed promise to their sister. 'Why don't you look in her tomb?' he suggested.

"The sisters were terrified, but they sought the help of relatives and, with lighted torches, down they went into the dank, stale crypt lined with coffins.

"There they pried open Anne's casket and found her corpse as they had buried it — fresh and undecayed. But severed from her body was her head — stripped of flesh and hair and the funeral flowers. The naked skull stood upright, gleaming in the light of the torches, grinning hideously at them, shadows flickering in the holes where eyes had been.

"'Aaaah!'" cried her eldest sister. 'It waits for us! We must honor her wish. . . . But I cannot . . . I cannot!'

"A stalwart uncle lifted Anne's grinning skull and carried it ahead of him into the hall, where he placed it on a table in the drawing room. There it remained for years. And nothing more was heard at night in Burton Agnes Hall.

"Generations later, another family took over the property. One of the new family refused to have the hideous skull remain, and ordered that it be buried in the garden. A young manservant dug a hole, dropped in the skull, and tamped the earth down.

"But as he beat upon the earth, the shrieking began again. Piteous, dying groans reverberated through every room of the manor house, just as they had centuries before.

"The new family went to bed, but none slept. Ooooooh, aaaaaaah! The inhuman moaning never ceased, hour after hour. When morning finally came, their garden was black from frost and all of their horses had mysteriously gone lame.

"'Aye, 'tis the will of Anne,' whispered an old manservant to his wife. 'I will fetch a spade and end the matter.' He went into the garden and dug up the skull, gently brushing mud from the gaping eye sockets. He dusted the bare, yellowed bone, and returned it to the hall.

"It sits there still, for all I know," said Aunt Morbelia. "A screaming skull will not rest. It forces us to do its bidding."

BOOOOM! sounded the lightning. Thunder and heavy rain beat down on the Fearings' house and yard.

"A screaming skull," Rocky murmured, eyes wide.

Todd had heard enough. He would have turned on

a nice, cheerful cartoon if his mom allowed TV on school days. As it was he said, "I'm going to the rec room to play pool."

Alan had made a little steeple out of his fingers. He was frowning at the steeple. "How do we know —" he began.

Erect and forbidding in her chair, Aunt Morbelia said, "*We* don't have to know. Others know, and that's enough."

"Can we come back tomorrow?" asked Rocky.

"Tomorrow I go to the learning center," Todd said. And maybe, for once, he wouldn't mind.

"Grab those candles from the dining room," he told Jeff. "Until the lights come on, the basement'll be like a cave."

"You mean a *grave*," Rocky intoned sepulchrally.

Aunt Morbelia rose from her chair. "First, get that fiend off my bed. And shut the door to my room, please."

6. Hanging In There

The next afternoon, as Todd headed down the walk to the learning center, Jeff called after him.

"I'll look for worms, okay? There'll be tons after yesterday's rain, so we can fish tonight."

"Right. See you then." Todd looked up briefly at a cloudless blue sky before he opened the door to the center.

Inside he went to Miss King's room. Since second grade, he had spent two afternoons a week in Room 104. He was "learning how to learn" as his teacher put it, and it was taking just short of forever.

He found his seat in the tiny classroom, nodded to Tanya and Jason, seventh-graders, and to Kevin, an eighth-grader. They, too, were dyslexic, and had been in class with him all along. Just a happy, carefree little group, he thought grimly.

From her desk Miss King asked, "Todd? Are you all right?"

Todd forced his head up. "Oh, sure."

Miss King pushed her chair back and stood up.

"Good. Then you can help me carry some stuff from the supply room."

Neither said anything until they were in the supply room. Then she spoke. "Okay, I lied. I don't need help. But I would like a reason for that long face you're wearing."

Todd shrugged. "Thanks, but nobody can help."

Miss King was taller than Todd only when she fluffed up her reddish hair. She could look him directly in the eyes and now she did.

"Is it this?" she asked, gesturing to include the whole building. "Coming here when you'd love to be doing something else? It's a perfect April day."

"Bingo." Todd looked out the narrow window.

"I wondered when you'd crack. All these years you've kept your temper in my class. Are you mad now?"

Todd jerked to attention. "Mad?"

"Yes. Red-hot furious. Why should you have dyslexia? Your friends don't. Is that fair? Is that justice?"

"No." But it was oddly comforting to have her say what he had thought so often. Of course he was furious. Who wouldn't be?

"Look, Todd, you have a right to be angry. Heave your language book to the floor and jump up and down on it."

"Yeah. I'd like to throw every reading book in the world into a giant bonfire. Voom! No more reading."

"That's the spirit! Get as mad as you can. I want you to fight. And you must believe you can win. Be-

cause if you don't fight and if you don't believe . . .
dyslexia will win. Until recently, it almost always did.

"Remember what I said about Thomas Edison?
How they sent him home from school with a note for
his mother saying he couldn't learn? And Rodin —
maybe the most famous sculptor ever born? And
Bruce Jenner, the Olympic gold-medalist in the de-
cathlon? You know how long I can go on listing brilliant, famous people."

"I know."

"Right. Now, one more thing. I saw your math papers from last week and you already understand con-
cepts that I don't, because I'm hopeless with figures.
But you'll be taking math at the high school next year,
did you know that?"

"You're kidding!"

She shook her head. "You and Alan Harriman.
You're both nearly finished with first-year algebra.
What would they do with you next year in seventh
grade?"

"It's crazy! I'm still reading like a turtle."

"You won't always be that way. Just growing older
will help a lot. You may always be a slow reader, but
you'll be miles ahead of them in math — and science,
too, according to your teachers. Just give me a few
more years, Todd. In the next few years, you'll see
real progress."

"Meanwhile I can spit on the books?"

"With my blessing. Now come on. We're going to
learn some new word roots today."

On their way back to class, Miss King asked, "Is your mom still working with you?"

"Yes. She reads every night, or Dad does. We've got Aunt Morbelia, too." Todd explained, telling her his aunt's idea for learning the months in order.

"Brilliant! I'll send some books home with you for her. She sounds like a gift from heaven."

Not quite, Todd thought wryly as he took his seat in class. His great-aunt had come from some other place. Still, Jeff and Alan and Rocky thought she was terrific. Rocky had already told most of the class about her storytelling and her homemade bread.

And that wasn't all. Rocky was using words like "fiend" and "ghoul" and "grinning skull." Amazing after only one afternoon, he thought. Luckily, he hadn't had a nightmare about the screaming skull. That one isn't too scary, he decided. But who knows what she'll say next? I wonder what she thinks about a creepy hooting owl?

"Todd?" Miss King called. "Yoo-hoo? It's either spit on the books or pay attention, all right?"

When Todd got home just before dinner, his mom, Inky, and Aunt Morbelia were gathered around the kitchen table. Banshee glowered down from atop the refrigerator.

"Oh, good," said Aunt Morbelia. "Maybe now Inky will transfer his attention to you."

Mrs. Fearing was dicing green peppers on a chopping board. She turned to Todd and said, "Inky is adopting Aunt Morbelia. I zip in and out, but he can count on her being right here — much too close to home, as I keep telling her, but Inky thinks it's wonderful."

By now, Inky was nudging Todd's leg. Todd set his books down and rubbed him all over. Inky's tongue lolled out, his eyes closed, and he danced with pleasure.

"That dog lives to be petted," observed Aunt Morbelia. "I must have washed my hands a hundred times today."

"You don't have to pet him every time he asks," Todd told her. "He can be sort of resistant."

"I think you mean *persistent*," said Todd's mother.

"Of course he does," Aunt Morbelia said quickly. "And what a perfect word to describe his behavior! Here, write it in the sauce." She shoved a long pan toward him with crust beneath a thick red sauce.

"Is this going to be pizza?" he asked.

"Yes, your mother is teaching me to make it. Now wash your hands and come back here, please."

Oh brother, he thought, scrubbing his hands in the sink. I'm sick of school! Can't anybody see that? He returned to the table, holding his clean hands out in front of him like a surgeon.

"See?" Aunt Morbelia wrote in the sauce with one long finger. "P-e-r-s-i-s-t. That is the word persistence comes from. Now you do it."

Todd wrote *persist* right below his aunt's letters.

"Lovely," she said. "Look at it hard, Todd. See the *per* in persist? The word has two parts, *per* and *sist*."

She shook the pan to smooth out the sauce and *persist* disappeared. "Now, see how many times you can fit it in."

Todd managed to write it six times. Miss King ought to be here, he thought, squeezing one more *persist* into a bit of undisturbed sauce. "I bet I remember it now," he said.

Aunt Morbelia was smiling. Not a suggestion, not a hint or a promise, but a real smile. "Excellent," she said, giving the word a new significance.

She shook the pan again. "Much easier than washing a blackboard," she said. And then they wrote *persistence*. They squeezed it in four times, but the last one looked like bird tracks. Owls, Todd thought.

"Aunt Morbelia, are owls unlucky?" he asked.

"Oh pooh," said his mother, shaking her head.

"Dreadful birds," said Aunt Morbelia. "It is always a bad omen to hear an owl hooting nearby. Someone in the family is likely to die soon."

When Aunt Morbelia went over to the sink, Todd's mom caught his eye and mouthed "Oh pooh!" again.

Todd nodded agreement, thinking of the times he had heard owls hoot in the night. There are only three in our family, he thought. If one had died, we'd have noticed.

Smiling at his own dark humor, Todd began filling

the pan with *persistence.* His dad came in and they explained what was going on.

"It looks like fun," said Mr. Fearing. "Is that dinner?"

"Yeah, Dad, if we ever quit playing with it."

"We are not finished," Aunt Morbelia said. She admired his work before shaking the pan again. Then she wrote *April, May, June.*

"Your turn," she said. "The flower months."

When he finished and had said the three new months several times without a slip, he said all six months that he knew — January through June. And again, and again. He wrote all six in pizza sauce.

His dad smiled. "Todd, if you decide to swim the ocean someday, we'll just sit back and say, Yup, he can do it."

"Don't get carried away," Todd said, pretending he didn't enjoy the praise. And now he knew — knew positively — six months in order! He would write the three flower months in his notebook, just in case, just as Miss King always insisted.

That thought reminded him of the books she'd sent home for his aunt. When he had washed off the pizza sauce, he gave them to her. And for the second time, he saw her smile.

"Oh, Todd," was all she said as she examined each book in turn. He had never seen anyone go all mushy over a few books. "I shall telephone to thank her. I cannot wait to read this material."

At that point Banshee had been patient long enough. She leapt from the refrigerator down to the counter, then to the floor, where she began stalking Aunt Morbelia's swaying skirts.

"Bad kitty," said Todd's mom, grabbing Banshee.

"Meeyow!"

Aunt Morbelia frowned. "That beast has taken a dislike to me," she said.

"Then you're even," replied Mr. Fearing. "Actually, I don't think she likes any of us. She generously allows us to feed her and give her a roof over her head."

"She likes to tease," Todd said. "I'll take her out." He took Banshee from his mother and went to the porch, where he sat down on the top step and held her on his lap.

"We can't keep putting you out," he whispered in one silken ear. "It isn't fair."

Fair. Boy, there was a word. Todd held his cat and loved her until the pizza was ready.

That evening, as Todd and Jeff sat on the end of the dock, their fishing lines in the water, Todd heard the hoot of an owl in the trees around the lake.

"Bad omen," Todd said, nodding over his shoulder at the woods behind them.

"Oh yeah? What now?"

"A hooting owl. Means somebody's going to die."

Jeff snorted. "Aunt Morbelia strikes again. You

think we should call my dad and tell him to rev up the hearse?"

They laughed together. "Do you think she really believes this stuff?" Todd asked. "At dinner she was carrying on about the crows on our lawn. You name it and it's bad luck."

"Yeah, but it's interesting. Her story was terrific. With that storm and no lights and her all in black and everything? I mean, nobody does that anymore, Todd!"

"No kidding!"

Jeff raised his pole and checked his bait. "How soon can we hear another story?" he asked.

"Oh, sometime," Todd answered, deliberately vague. After all, no one knew how long his aunt would stay. She was supposed to be "trying it out," that's all.

But she was not a person who would blend subtly into the background of his life. She was noticeable, even when she didn't mean to be. Like Banshee.

And wouldn't Aunt Morbelia just *love* that comparison, he thought, amused.

7. Todd Tells a Story

Todd wrote *May 15* on his paper and thought, Yay! Summer's coming. Time was jumping along this spring.

Often after school his friends came to hear Aunt Morbelia tell a story . . . and to eat homemade rolls or bread. The Hampshire librarian had always read books aloud, but those were baby stories compared to his great-aunt's scarifying tales.

When he wasn't being the host of the new "entertainment center," as his mom called their house, he was in school or in class with Miss King, studying with Aunt Morbelia, or playing outdoors.

Now, he was definitely indoors and unhappy. He frowned down at his blank paper, thinking how much he hated in-class writing assignments. He could never think of a good idea under pressure. Even if he did, he wouldn't have enough time and he couldn't spell half the words he wanted to use.

Also, he was tired. He had had another nightmare,

this time about a grisly thing that had risen eerily out of the creek at the back of his yard. It was a man — hacked in half at the waist!

Todd had watched, terrified and frozen in his dream, as the two bleeding parts started toward his house. The top half had spooky white eyes under dark, stringy hair. He wore a leather thong round his neck and a stained cream-colored shirt. His bottom half wore brown trousers with tall leather boots.

Side by side, dripping bright red blood on the spring green grass, the halves oozed toward him through a swirling mist. Nearer and nearer came the gruesome body parts. When the top half reached for the door to his house, Todd had wakened, a scream in his throat. His pajamas were soaked with sweat.

Now, remembering, he felt his forehead sweating again. Geez! he thought. Mom's right. I have too much imagination.

Oh yeah? teased his mind. That's why you do so well on these papers, huh? Your great imagination?

Todd put his head down on the blank paper. Maybe he could say he didn't feel well. It wouldn't be a lie.

Mr. Darnell, the language-arts teacher, sauntered down the aisle and stopped beside him. "Problem?" he whispered.

Now was his chance. "You wouldn't believe the nightmare I had last night," he whispered back. "I hardly slept at all and now I can't think."

"Okay," Mr. Darnell said, "tell me that nightmare.

If you want to unload one of those things, this's the best way. Gets it out of your system. Besides, it'll be a great paper."

"You sure?"

Mr. Darnell nodded. "I had horrible nightmares as a kid. They scared me silly. Just try it, all right?"

"I guess so." Todd picked up his pencil as Mr. Darnell resumed his classroom stroll. It was odd to think of his teacher having nightmares — Mr. Darnell, who looked like a football tackle. Todd enjoyed him. He had worked harder for him than he had for any other English teacher.

Now he closed his eyes and tried to think of a good title while he cleaned his eraser on his jeans. He used an eraser in this class more than anyone he knew, and he didn't want smudges to mess up his paper.

Carefully, on the top line, he printed, "The Bloody Man of Hampshire." He checked each word letter by letter.

Half an hour later everyone else had finished and the lunch bell rang. Todd looked up. He was only partly finished and this was going to be his best story.

"Can I finish after school?" he called to Mr. Darnell.

"Class, quiet!" ordered the teacher. To Todd he said, "Certainly. Meet you here at three."

A few days later, Mr. Darnell passed back the in-class writing assignments. Todd did not get his back.

Mr. Darnell stood in front of the class and said, "I want to read you a particularly vivid paper."

Todd looked around to see who else hadn't gotten a paper. He knew it wouldn't be his story. No one had ever read one of his aloud.

"The Bloody Man of Hampshire," began the teacher in his deep, strong voice.

"Hey! Way to go!" said Jeff, one cheering fist raised in the air. He knew whose paper it was.

"Shhh," said Mr. Darnell. "You're mucking up the mood, Jeff, and this is a terrific story."

Todd felt his face grow warm. Even his ears were hot. He stared down at his desk, knowing that the whole class was watching him. This time it was okay.

When Mr. Darnell finished reading, everybody clapped and Todd blushed again. His story had sounded really great when the teacher read it. And now, somehow, that's all it was. Just a story. Something he'd made up.

"This was an interesting set of papers," Mr. Darnell said. "I got half a dozen ghost stories. Is there a new movie in town that I don't know about?"

Several kids giggled. "It's Aunt Morbelia," Rocky announced. "She lives at Todd's house."

Todd had to explain Aunt Morbelia again.

"How fortunate," commented Mr. Darnell when Todd finished. "For years, storytelling has been a lost art, but now it's being revived. I think we have a real artist right here in town. Todd, would your aunt talk to our class?"

"I don't know," he said. "She stays home a lot. She's been to the library a few times, and yesterday she went shopping with Mom, but . . . I just don't know."

"With your permission, I'd like to call and ask her," Mr. Darnell said.

"Fine," he said. "She's all yours."

Class resumed. The kids reported to their "fix-it" groups, as Mr. Darnell called them, to correct the errors on their papers. As usual, Alan was the head of Todd's group.

"Did you look at this?" Alan asked, peering through his heavy glasses at Todd's paper. "I think it's better. Not tons, but better. See?"

Todd examined the three pages that had taken so long to write. Here and there was a line with only one spelling error — or none! Other sentences had two or three mistakes. But yes, it was better.

He looked up at Alan. "Next time," he said, being careful not to smile, "I should be the head of this group."

Alan grinned appreciatively.

When school was out, Todd left Jeff at the sidewalk leading to the learning center. "I'll just be a minute," he said. "Meet you at your house later, okay?"

Todd hurried up the steps and was opening the door to the center when he saw who was on the inside. Aunt Morbelia. She was unmistakable.

The door whuffed shut behind him and he stood still, not knowing what to say.

"Hello, Todd," she said. "This is not one of your regular afternoons, is it?"

"No, but I need to see Miss King."

"I just came from seeing her. I was returning the books she lent me and thanking her. I liked her very much." Aunt Morbelia paused, arranging the white cuffs of her blouse below the black jacket sleeves before she went on.

"She thinks I should do volunteer work here. Is that not amazing? I told her I was too old, of course."

Whoa, Todd thought. Aunt Morbelia at home, Aunt Morbelia at school telling stories, Aunt Morbelia in my learning center. Give me a break.

Except there was something in her voice when she had said "too old, of course." He knew better. Too weird, maybe. Too superstitious, you bet. But not too old to teach. Then she was a different person.

And she was looking at him now with those powerful eyes, waiting for a response.

"That'd be good," he said finally. "I mean, Miss King is right. And Mom keeps saying you ought to get out and do things." Yeah, he thought. Maybe she'd be *here* sometimes when I'm home. I don't hate her or anything, but lately I can't seem to avoid her.

"Yup," he said, mind made up, "that's a cool idea. You're a really good teacher."

She tilted her head, considering him. "Thank you, Todd. I value your opinion. But the school year is almost over and they have done fine without me here."

"Yeah, but their big time is summer. Lots of kids come every morning — kids from other towns, too. Well, I'm going to Jeff's today, okay? See you later."

"Good afternoon, Todd."

He watched her erect figure turn and go through the door and down the wide steps to the sidewalk. She'd have made a great queen, he thought.

In Miss King's room, he simply laid his paper on her desk. She looked at the "A" at the top, then up at him. "The first one," she said. "Bless Mr. Darnell for getting the message and overlooking the errors."

"We have to fix the mixtakes. If we fix them all, they don't count. I have to turn it in again tomorrow."

"That's a fine idea." She stood up and held out her hand. "To the first of many good English papers. Probably not in a row — not all at once — but there'll be more."

"I sure hope so," he said as they shook hands.

"Just stay fighting mad," she said, smiling as she sat back down at her desk. "And try to talk your aunt into being a volunteer here. It'd be good for her and wonderful for us. Your writing words in pizza sauce was one of the best ideas I've heard in years."

"It was fun. And she didn't even know we used fingerpaint or sand here. Nobody told her that."

Miss King nodded. "Yes, she has a gift. Be glad she brought it to your house."

On the way to Jeff's, Todd thought about what Miss King had said. He was supposed to be glad Aunt Morbelia had come to live at his house. Well, he was and he wasn't. He didn't want his friends coming over just to hear her stories and eat her baked goods. He was sick of creepy stories. He hated nightmares and worrying about when he'd have another one.

But she always kept him company when he did his homework. He liked working with her. And he loved hot sweet rolls and fresh bread. . . .

He was still listing Aunt Morbelia's pluses and minuses when he got to Jeff's house.

"Come on in!" Jeff hollered when Todd called through the Lorimers' screen door. "I've got an idea!"

8. Good Luck, Bad Luck

Todd followed the sound of Jeff's voice back to the Lorimers' family room. Jeff was working on a model plane to add to his collection.

"Pretty classy," Todd commented when he saw it.

"It's a World War II Flying Tiger," Jeff said, admiring the propeller he had cemented into place. "It has these really cool teeth on both sides of the engine compartment. See?" He pointed to the diagram. "It'd be fun to fly one, but I won't get to. It's all jets now. Tons of instruments."

Todd nodded. "Yup. No challenge." He watched as Jeff cemented another piece into place. "So what's your idea?"

Jeff laid his tweezers down on the page of model directions. "It just came to me while I was sitting here." He lowered his voice. "Let's be ghosts, okay? Think of the kids we could scare — like Rocky."

"Live people can't be ghosts, gerbil-brain."

"They do it in movies all the time! See, we wait for a real foggy night, maybe kind of rainy, and we get

66

some of that curtainy, see-through material to hide under. And no shoes. Ghosts don't wear shoes."

"Uh-huh," Todd said, beginning to get the idea, imagining himself under the gauzy curtain fabric. "No clothes, either. They'd show through."

"Go naked?" Jeff yelped.

"No-o-o," Todd said slowly, shaking his head. "We'd wear something that looked like skin, sort of tan or pinky." And then he remembered.

"I've got it! At home. The perfect stuff."

"So tell me!" Jeff was bouncing in his chair.

"Mom made a mistake in the wash and turned some of my underwear this barfy pink color. Nobody'd wear it — no way — but it's perfect."

Jeff's smile stretched nearly ear to ear. "Yeah! And we should have spooky-colored hands to stick out in front of us. We can use Dad's corpse makeup. It's great stuff."

"It is?" Todd said, wondering about the words on an undertaker's cosmetic supplies. Surely not "Lively Pink" or "Rise 'n' Shine Red" as on his mom's makeup.

Jeff said, "Yup, we're all set. I'll watch the weather, okay? You get the ghost material from your mom's office."

Todd thought of his mother's piles of sample fabrics. "Yeah, but if we mess it up, I'm burned, you know that."

"No problem, no problem," Jeff said hastily.

When Todd and Jeff sat down to dinner later, they had planned exactly how to haunt Hampshire. Jeff sent one hungry look around the table and said, "Oh, good, gaspetti!"

"Ah, come on," Todd said. "I can say it now. Spaghetti. Spaghetti. See?"

Mr. Lorimer chuckled. "Nice, Todd, but no fun. We never call it spaghetti anymore. Here, have some garlic bread."

Jeff's oldest brother, Jim, said, "Words must be getting easier for you, Todd. It's been years since you said anything good like 'hackyturctor' instead of helicopter."

"Hackyturctor — the *all-time great word*," Jeff declared solemnly, as if he were bestowing a medal.

"Thank you, thank you." Todd bowed right and left.

Jeff's fourteen-year-old brother, Duane, pointed his fork at Todd. "Is your aunt real tall, and does she wear old-fashioned clothes — all black? I think I saw her on your street this afternoon."

"Duane, your fork is for eating, not for pointing," said Mrs. Lorimer before she turned to Todd. "How is your aunt? Is she still so full of depressing forecasts?"

Todd tried to decide. "Well," he said, feeling all the Lorimer eyes upon him, "sometimes she is, but not always.

"She was pretty funny this morning," he went on. "Dad said he felt lousy and maybe he was getting the flu, so Aunt Morbelia said he should take a bath and throw the water over the cat, and then he'd get better."

That broke everyone up. When Mr. Lorimer stopped laughing, he asked, "Is that a remedy for illness?"

"I guess so, but it's a good thing Banshee didn't hear her. I sure hope nobody at our house gets very sick."

By the end of the meal, Todd felt as if he had been a guest speaker. Jeff's family couldn't seem to hear enough about Aunt Morbelia.

"I'm going to have some women here for a welcome party," declared Mrs. Lorimer. "Your aunt's obviously got a dozen talents. If I can get her involved in local projects, she'll have better things to think about."

Dinner over, Jeff said, "Come on, Todd. Let's bike out to the park and see who's there."

"Probably just a few owls, maybe some crows," Todd said as they carried their plates to the sink. Both of them chortled.

"Now, boys," Mr. Lorimer said in his father voice, "people still have lots of superstitions. Nothing hangs on like a good superstition." He finished wiping Princess's hands and lifted her out of her high chair.

"You guys be home by dark, hear? I'll call your dad, Todd, and tell him where you are."

Todd spent the next afternoon in Miss King's class, but the following day, Rocky was waiting for him at his locker after school.

"I want to hear another story," she said. "So all of us are going home with you, okay?"

Not okay, he thought, but he knew it was hopeless. When Rocky made up her mind, she was a steamroller.

"I guess," he said, resigned. "You get Alan and I'll find Jeff." And you can hear a story, he thought, while the rest of us do something fun — the way we always used to, he thought, watching her dart away to look for Alan.

Within seconds of their arrival at Todd's house, everyone had petted Inky, and Rocky was hanging over the chair where Aunt Morbelia sat reading a book. "Aunt Morbelia," Rocky began demurely, "it's been days since I heard a really good story. That's too bad, don't you think?"

Todd's aunt looked up from her book. "Do you feel exceptionally deprived?" she asked.

Todd grinned. Although his aunt wasn't smiling, he was getting better at reading her face and tone of voice. He was sure she was smiling inside.

But she had fooled Rocky, who clearly didn't know what to say next.

"She's asking for another story," Todd said.

"That's rude," Rocky said, chin high. "I was just sort of working up to it.

"But would you tell one, please?" she begged, plunking herself on the floor next to Inky at Aunt Morbelia's feet. "And I need to know what to do when something bad happens. Maybe some magic spells or potions? I want to know *all* the bad stuff — about hooting owls and black cats —"

"You guys want to get up a ball game?" Todd asked Alan and Jeff.

Aunt Morbelia closed her book. "I think we should discuss things that everyone is interested in, don't you?"

"That's cool," said Jeff. "Are there any more good-luck things like making wishes when an eyelash is on your cheek, and four-leaf clovers? Stuff like that."

"Why, of course," said Aunt Morbelia. "Lots of things are good omens. There are even helpful ghosts."

"Who cares?" Rocky said. "They aren't interesting."

"They are, too!" chorused Todd and Jeff.

"Now, children," Alan joked.

Aunt Morbelia held up one hand. "Let us try a bit of both, all right? First, spells and potions. Rocky, I do not know about those things. Witches do, I suspect, but not I.

"However, the sign of the cross is the most common way to chase away bad luck. And, let us see . . . If you stumble, you may snap your fingers for better luck. If you want to make a wish, step over a ladder while you wish, and it is supposed to come true." She leaned forward. "Smile at me, Rocky."

Rocky smiled, though not comfortably.

"I thought so," said Aunt Morbelia. "Widely spaced teeth mean you will travel a great deal, and be prosperous and happy."

"It's her dentist who'll be prosperous and happy,"

Todd said. "Mine are like that, too, and Mom says it's going to cost a fortune to have them fixed."

Rocky was frowning.

"Ooh, never frown like that, Rocky, dear," said Aunt Morbelia. "It makes ugly lines on your forehead — makes you look old before your time."

Rocky stopped frowning.

"Now let me see," Aunt Morbelia went on, "some more old beliefs . . ." She was quiet a moment.

She called them "old beliefs," Todd thought. Maybe she doesn't believe in them either. They're just what she knows. Something old and familiar.

For the first time he thought of how little she had brought with her. A few suitcases of clothes, some boxes of books, and the two pictures of her ancestors. Yet she and her sisters had kept house for years. She left almost everything behind, he decided.

Todd realized she was talking again.

". . . and if you make a face when the clock is striking twelve, your face may stay that way. . . . Oh, and here is another. If you see something frightening, you say, 'Crisscross, double-cross. Tell the monster to get lost.'"

"I love that," said Rocky, hanging on every word.

"Because it is different," Aunt Morbelia replied. "New information is always interesting, don't you think?"

"Especially ghost stories," insisted Rocky.

Todd said, "Come on, you guys, let's *do* something."

"You're right, Todd." Aunt Morbelia stood up. "Time to weed the flower beds. Does anyone want to help?"

"I will, if you'll tell me a story," Rocky said.

Alan shook his head. "I can't. I have to pick up a book for my dad at the library. See you guys tomorrow."

And so, for the first time in years, Rocky did not go looking for a ball game with Todd and Jeff. She went to the garden with Aunt Morbelia.

On the way to the park Todd asked, "Have you heard a weather forecast?"

"Huh?" answered Jeff. "Oh, yeah — our big night! Nah, just sunshine. Sorry."

"I can't wait for rain," Todd said. "Rocky's being a pain in the butt. She needs ghosts, all right. In her own backyard!"

"Her bedroom's right above it, too," exulted Jeff. "It's perfect, just perfect!"

9. Ghosts in the Classroom

Near the end of May, Todd found it harder and harder to study in the evenings. He would sit at the kitchen table and hear bugs fluttering against the screen and kids yelling close by — normal kids whose schoolwork ended at three o'clock.

He was staring out the window one evening at a large tan moth and thinking how easy it would be to be a moth, when he heard the sound of Aunt Morbelia's skirts. He felt rather than saw her sit down across from him.

"Your friends are all playing outdoors, aren't they?"

"Sure," he said, turning toward her and away from the window. "They're not like me."

"I know. Todd, I have been wondering about something. Have you always done homework at night, after dinner?"

"Lots of nights, yeah. Not every one."

"But you are a morning person as I am — and your father."

"Morning's nice. I feel good then."

74

"What if you did homework early — first thing — and played outdoors after dinner?"

"Yeah," he said. "Homework before breakfast!"

"Exactly. Shall we meet in the morning at six-thirty? We can do your homework and start learning the hot months — July, August, and September."

"Sure!" he said as his parents came in the door, debating the merits of a new car. Inky followed them in, going first to Todd, then to Aunt Morbelia. He sat down on her skirt hem.

The noise of Todd's parents' debate woke Banshee, who yowled, then came toward them, tail thrashing.

Aunt Morbelia gathered up her skirts, jerking part of the material from under Inky's haunches. "Just stay away," she warned, one long finger pointed at the cat.

"Oh dear," said Todd's mother, forgetting about the new car. "Is she still pestering you?"

"Yes. She has been in the same room with me all day. First thing this morning she was sniffing the towel over my rising dough. When I shooed her off the counter, she wrapped herself around my ankles. I have had to watch every step I took this livelong day."

As if she understood, Banshee minced over to Aunt Morbelia and sat down, her body touching the glossy black shoe. Aunt Morbelia moved her foot. Banshee moved her bottom — just enough to remain in contact. She wrapped her silken tail round her paws and gazed up at Aunt Morbelia.

"Hrrr," rumbled Inky, head lowered.

Banshee didn't even look at him. Eyes on Aunt Morbelia, she meowed softly.

Aunt Morbelia drew herself up and glared down at the offender. When Banshee didn't flinch, she turned to Todd. "Why is this animal defying me?"

"She's decided she likes you," he replied, wanting to laugh and knowing it was not the time.

"I beg your pardon?" snapped Aunt Morbelia.

Mr. Fearing was trying unsuccessfully to hide a smile. "Yes, ma'am," he said. "I agree with Todd. She's never acted that way with us — unless she's starving. I think she's finally found someone she approves of."

"An animal always knows," said Todd's mother.

And Todd knew his cat. She's jealous of the attention Inky's getting, he decided. And she's ticked off because Aunt Morbelia ignores her. Oh boy. I don't know a stubborner animal than Banshee.

Because he couldn't think of anything better, Todd said, "Just pretend you don't see her, okay?"

"Yes," agreed Mrs. Fearing. "At least she's black, so her hairs won't show on your clothes. But . . . as I said the other day . . . I wish you'd consider a different color, Morbelia. You'd be lovely in a dove gray, or perhaps mauve. You'd be simply handsome in mauve."

"Black will do, thank you. It would be unthinkable to dress otherwise for the year following Cordelia's death. Besides, black suits me."

Inky stopped eyeing Banshee and put his head on Aunt Morbelia's knee.

Aunt Morbelia looked down into the dog's face. "He has the most expressive eyes," she said, "but I do not understand why he is attracted to me." She lay one hand on Inky's head and let it rest there quietly.

"He knows you're part of his family," said Todd's mom. "That's how dogs are. Inky loves all of us — unconditionally. He doesn't expect us to be perfect and he asks very little. We took him in and so he loves us."

She bent over and kissed Inky's head and he turned to lick her cheek.

"I can't imagine life without a dog," Todd's mother concluded, rising. "Well, I'd better get busy. I have to make something for the fire company's bake sale tomorrow."

"Why didn't you tell me?" said Aunt Morbelia. "I could easily have managed a cake or a pie this afternoon."

"Thank you, Morbelia, but I want to do my part."

"Well, I can help," Aunt Morbelia insisted. She gave Inky one last pat and Banshee a final frown. When she headed for the sink, Banshee followed, chasing the swaying skirt and batting at it with one paw.

"This town certainly needs volunteers," said Aunt Morbelia, twitching her skirt away from the cat. "Today they begged me to help at the library, and they barely know me."

As the adults talked, Todd piled up his books. "Mom, I'm going out."

"Is your homework finished?" she asked.

His aunt answered for him. "We are going to work in the mornings from now on. Bright and early."

"Oh, pew," said Mrs. Fearing, making a face. "I'm a night person myself. All right, Todd, but be home before nine. Dad's reading tonight and you know how sleepy he gets."

Todd whistled to Inky and the two dashed outside before any more precious time was lost. Already he liked the new study schedule. Spring evenings were meant for play.

The next day, with sun on the kitchen table and orange juice at his right hand, Todd opened his notebook.

Aunt Morbelia sat down across from him and stirred milk into her coffee. "Good morning," she said. "Would you say the first six months, please?"

Todd gave her January through June, no mistakes.

"Now write the hot months: July, August, September."

He practiced the hot months several times, writing them and saying them out loud. "Now from the top," he announced, full of confidence.

But it didn't work. Somehow, nine months were a lot more than six. As he was saying the first six, he'd think of keeping the three new months in order, and one of them would end up in the wrong place.

Miss King had promised progress was coming. But when? How many years? Todd wanted to cry and yell and tear his notebook into a zillion pieces. He could feel his face getting redder by the second.

"Stop," ordered his aunt. "I am not teaching this correctly or we would be doing better. It is too soon to say all of them in order. We shall work only with the three new months." Softly she chanted, "July, August, September."

"July, August, September," Todd repeated through clenched teeth. And again, and again. And then he pounded the table. "It's not fair! It's just not fair!"

Aunt Morbelia put her hand over his fist. "No, it is not," she said. "Life is not fair. No one ever promised that it would be. But you will learn to say the months, Todd. We will find a way. Now look at me and repeat, 'I will learn to say the months.'"

Todd raised his head and mumbled, "I will learn to say the months."

"Louder."

"I will learn to say the months!"

"Shout."

"I WILL LEARN TO SAY THE MONTHS!"

"Excellent," she said. "I believe you now. Let me pop the bread in the oven and we shall begin your homework." She stood up. "I have been invited to a meeting at the learning center today, did you know that?"

Todd shook his head.

"I do not know why they included me, but I found

it impossible to refuse Miss King. Also, I shall be in your class today as a guest speaker, remember?"

"Is it today?" Todd felt his anger gradually ebb away. Even if he hated ghost stories, it'd be good to have a classroom guest. Something different.

"All right," she said, sitting back down at the table. "Let us look at your homework for today."

Aunt Morbelia entered Todd's classroom at 10:30, just when language arts usually began. Todd cheered silently as her regal figure crossed the room. He felt the absolute silence in her wake and thought, I'm sure kids never acted up in her class.

Mr. Darnell moved his chair to the front of the room. With a formal bow, he invited Aunt Morbelia to take a seat.

"Please welcome Todd's aunt, Miss Morbelia Fearing," he said. "She knows many fascinating things, and I hope you'll give her your complete attention."

Not to worry, Todd thought. His class was mesmerized by the black-suited figure in the chair.

"I hear that you are interested in . . . ghosts," began Aunt Morbelia. Her peculiar emphasis on the word *ghosts* sent shivers through her listeners. "Well, I grew up with ghosts — not all of them human. In Yorkshire we fear the dog of Satan, Black Shuck.

"Bigger than a calf is Black Shuck," said Aunt Morbelia, unmoving in her chair, as if she were a speaking statue.

"His eyes glow red as Satan's fire and he comes out

of nowhere, an enormous beast, racing through the dark night on silent paws. Once he came to Rufus of Northmoor — an evil, yellow-eyed man who lived in a stone hut on the edge of the village.

"They say that Rufus had a wife at one time. A poor, driven slave she was, working their little farm while Rufus drank at the pubs in town. One day she collapsed in the fields. No one knows how long she lay there, but when passersby found her, she was stone cold. Rufus let the town bury her and that very night he set off to drink as usual.

"But now Black Shuck came out of the dark and followed him. Rufus flew down the road in fear, but always, just over his shoulder, he saw the huge hellhound, eyes burning, right behind him.

"When Rufus finally staggered into the pub, he was too terrified to talk, and he shook continuously.

"'Black hound of hell,' gibbered Rufus at last. 'Dun know whurr he come from. Red devil eyes he has and he's atter me, he is. He's atter me! I ain' a-goin' out there again, nossir. I ain' niver goin' out there na more!'

"The publican let Rufus drink until he passed out on the floor of the pub. He hired men to take Rufus home in a wagon and put him inside his stone hut.

"After that, those who lived on the moors nearby saw Black Shuck in the night, always by the hut of Rufus. Sometimes he sat right outside, his fiery eyes fixed on the door. Sometimes he paced round and round the hut.

"Rufus did not step outside. No one would go near because they knew about Black Shuck. Days, then weeks, passed. Townspeople saw Rufus look out a window from time to time in the day — his yellow eyes wide with fright. But he never came out of doors. And no one went near.

"'Black Shuck was on the moors again tonight,' said an old man. 'He's waiting for Rufus to die.'

"You see, they knew Rufus would starve all alone in his hut. But no one dared to go there.

"And then came a day when people said to one another, 'It howled on the moors last night. Did you hear it? The most dreadful sound! Heaven help us!'

"After that, no one saw Rufus look out his window. And no one saw or heard Black Shuck at night.

"At last, the sheriff and his men went to Rufus's hut on a brave, sunshiny day. They took the big wooden cross from the church and they held silver crosses out in front of them to ward off the devil dog, even though it was day.

"When they got to the hut, they found its door open, creaking mournfully back and forth. And inside . . . inside . . . *nothing*. Two chairs, an ancient bedstead, empty cupboards. On the floor near the bed lay the clothes of Rufus — filthy rags in the shape of a body.

"But there was no body. It had vanished altogether. Still, we know," whispered Aunt Morbelia. "We know what happened to Rufus of Northmoor."

Silence.

So that's a hellhound, Todd thought. And Inky really does look like one. The comparison between him and Black Shuck made Todd smile.

Mr. Darnell began to clap. Everyone joined in and the spell was broken. Students shifted in their seats. Some leaned over to whisper to friends.

A few sneezed with spring allergies and blew their noses. Sound by sound, the room returned to normal.

Aunt Morbelia raised one hand and the sounds stopped. "I am hearing sneezes," she said. "Did anyone sneeze before breakfast today?"

Several hands snaked upward, their owners looking around the room uneasily.

"A sneeze before breakfast means that you will get a present sometime this week," said Aunt Morbelia. "Also, three sneezes in a row are good luck . . . and there is an old rhyme about sneezing. This is how it goes:

Sneeze on Monday, sneeze for danger;
Sneeze on Tuesday, kiss a stranger;
Sneeze on Wednesday, get a letter;
Sneeze on Thursday, something better;
Sneeze on Friday, sneeze for sorrow;
Sneeze on Saturday, see your sweetheart tomorrow.
Sneeze on Sunday, your safety seek,
Or the Devil will have you all the week."

Nice, Todd thought, except I don't believe there's a devil with horns and a pointy tail.

Rocky raised her hand. "That's cool," she said, "but can you tell us another scary story?"

Todd groaned. He leaned across the aisle to whisper to Jeff. "What's the matter with the weather? Why isn't it raining?"

"You got me," Jeff muttered. "Darnell's looking at us, pea-brain."

Todd sat up straight, eyes to the front.

"I think one story is sufficient for today," Aunt Morbelia was saying. "But you may wish to ask questions about ghosts."

Alan's hand shot up. "Why do some people become ghosts and not others? We don't have any ghosts in my family."

"That is a good question, Alan. A ghost is an uneasy spirit — often a person seeking revenge for a terrible wrong, such as murder. The spirit keeps coming back until the guilty one is punished. Then it can rest. Sometimes a ghost will punish members of an evil family for generations.

"Of course, there are benevolent ghosts who return to earth to warn loved ones of danger or to deliver a message. And there is much we do not understand. In several experiments now, people are trying to communicate with the spirits of the dead."

Who needs that? Todd thought, shuddering.

Mr. Darnell stepped forward. "The lunch bell is going to ring and we'll have to stop now. But first, let's have a round of applause for the best storyteller I've ever heard."

Aunt Morbelia stayed for lunch and ate with Mr. Darnell and other teachers. Todd glanced at their table off and on and could see that his aunt was having a good time.

At his own table, he heard Rocky telling kids another of his aunt's ghost stories. Rocky had ghosts on the brain.

"If we don't get some bad weather pretty soon," he told Jeff, "we'll just do it anyway, okay?" He nodded his head in Rocky's direction. "She's driving me bats."

10. The Hampshire Haunting

The rain came early in June. As Todd sat down to his morning homework, he heard the first drops plop onto the leaves of the sycamore near the kitchen window. He saw the solid gray skies and rejoiced.

"Hold on," he told his aunt. "I have to call Jeff."

When Jeff came sleepily on the line, Todd said, "Look outside! And it's a *Friday*, get it?" And I can't say any more, he thought, because my aunt will get real suspicious.

"Hunh? Hey, Todd, do you know what time it is?"

Uh-oh, he thought, wishing again that he paid more attention to time. "Sorry . . . but *it's raining.* Don't you think it'd be a good idea if I slept over at your place?"

"Oh yeah," Jeff said, catching on. "Right!"

Todd was jubilant when he sat back down at the table. At last they were going to fix Rocky. Once she'd been really scared, she'd give up ghosts and return to normal.

Aunt Morbelia said nothing about the phone call.

She slid large, blank pieces of paper toward him and said, "Please write July at the top, August under it, then September, in order, and in great big letters."

Todd forced himself to concentrate. In huge letters he wrote the three hot months on several pieces of paper.

While he worked, his aunt pulled a mixing bowl out of the refrigerator and turned on the oven. As soon as Todd had finished, she said, "Do you like sugar cookies?"

"For breakfast?" Stay asleep, Mom, he prayed.

"Breakfast today, yes, but I should keep that a secret if I were you. After today, they will be dessert."

Fascinated, Todd joined her at the butcher-block table in the center of the kitchen and watched as she rolled the chilled dough into long, slender pencils. She pinched off one length and made a J, then a U, an L, and a Y.

She stood back, eyeing the pan, then said, "No. We shall do it smaller, in cursive letters. Watch me once, and then you can make lots of July cookies."

The kitchen soon filled with the aroma of July baking in the oven. August followed, and September, in delicious, fragrant odor.

Mr. Fearing's voice reached them before he appeared in the kitchen. "I don't know what it is, but I can hardly wait," he said, rounding the corner.

"You get to eat three at a time — in order — and don't tell Mom," said Todd.

"Of course not," said his dad, popping a hot July into his mouth. "I'm no fool." He planted a sugary kiss on Aunt Morbelia's cheek. "Brilliant, my dear. And what do you plan to do with the rest of your day? This'll be hard to top."

Pink from the oven's heat and her success, Aunt Morbelia smiled at him over a panful of September. "I shall be the guest of honor at Mrs. Lorimer's coffee hour this morning," she said. "A most thoughtful idea, especially for a busy young mother."

Todd stopped shaping the last September to look at his aunt's face. She's getting happy, he thought.

"Rroof! Rrooof!"

"Merowrrr!"

Aunt Morbelia's expression changed.

"I'll let them in," Todd said. "They don't like rain." He opened the door and Banshee scooted in. She sat down on the mat and began to groom her fur.

Inky bounded in over the top of her, trotted to the middle of the kitchen, and shook himself from ears to tail, generously sprinkling the room.

"Inky!" cried Aunt Morbelia.

Inky's head and ears drooped. He dropped to his belly and slunk under the kitchen table. From there he peered woefully up at Aunt Morbelia.

"Oh, dear," she said.

"No problem," Todd assured her. "I'll wipe him off and he'll be fine." He grabbed a towel and whistled to Inky.

Inky crawled out from under the table and sat up, squirming happily as Todd rubbed his thick coat. He gave Todd's ear a thorough washing with his tongue.

"Well, for once, the cat knows how to behave," said Aunt Morbelia. "Why is that dog cleaning your ear instead of his own body?"

Mr. Fearing said, "Because he's a dog, that's why. Come on, Todd. We'd better have some juice and cereal. I'll drop you off at school. It's pouring out there."

Friday lasted longer than most Fridays. Todd and Jeff could hardly wait for night. When school was out, Todd ran home to pack.

As he stepped into the kitchen, Aunt Morbelia said, "Tell me the hot months."

"July, August, September." He grinned. "I've got them for sure. I said them all day. Listen to this." He set his books down, closed his eyes, and chanted, "January, February, March. April, May, June. July, August, September!"

Aunt Morbelia smiled as she had that morning. "Well done," she said. "We shall simply stay with these months for a while . . . and enjoy them."

"Right," Todd agreed, afraid of adding the last three months and being mixed up again. It was such a hopeless, frustrating feeling. He could never explain it to others.

"I'm going to Jeff's now. Is Mom home?"

"She is at someone's house hanging draperies. I have the number if you need to call her."

No way, he thought. He had been dreaming up excuses to get his mother out of her office while he borrowed two fabric samples, but now it would be easy.

"I'll just throw some stuff in a bag," Todd told his aunt. "Mom knows where I'm going."

Todd packed quickly and left for Jeff's house. After dinner, he and Jeff watched a rented movie with the Lorimers and then said good night. "See you in the morning," Jeff hollered as they shut his door.

Todd crouched by the window and looked out. It was foggy, damp, gloomy — made to order. He and Jeff waited for silence to settle on the house. And finally, after having imagined it for so long, the time came to go haunting.

They put on the flesh pink underwear first. "Sure is perfect," Jeff said. "So's this material."

"Yeah, and it has to stay like that, remember?"

"I know. I've got a surprise. Close your eyes." Jeff reached under his bed and pulled out a human skull. "Okay, you can look now."

"Geez!" Todd squawked, jumping back.

"Looks real, huh? My very own screaming skull. See, I was looking at plane models, and there it was on the counter! They wouldn't let me buy theirs, so I bought the kit."

"It looks real, all right. You ready now?"

Very slowly, Jeff opened his window and slid up the screen. "It's just a few feet — only be quiet."

They dropped to the porch roof, slid down a column to the porch railing, then hopped to its floor. On bare, silent feet they tiptoed down the steps and zipped across the yard.

Behind the garage, they unfolded the gauzy curtain fabric and draped it over their bodies. "Here's the makeup," Jeff said, handing Todd a tube.

The tube read, "Base White." How boring, Todd thought. I was sure it'd say, "Healthy Old Female" or "Outdoorsman Red" — something undertakery.

He rubbed the makeup on his hands and face before pulling an old white bathing cap over his hair. He was spooky white from head to ankles.

"Perfect!" whispered Jeff. Head covered with his material, carrying his skull in front of him, Jeff nodded to Todd and they set off for Rocky's house through the backyards of Hampshire.

"So, now what?" Jeff asked when they were standing near a tall hedge leading into Rocky's yard.

Todd picked up gravel from the driveway. "We wake her up, beagle-brain." He aimed at Rocky's window and began pelting it with gravel. Chink. Chink. Chink.

"There she is!" hissed Jeff, pointing at the window.

"Shh!" Todd stood still for a second, then began walking across the open yard. He tried to float, like a proper ghost.

"Row-sa-Lynnn," he moaned, hands out in front of him. "Row-sa-Lynnnnn. Unnnnnnh." What a terrific groan, he thought. He did it again and again, intensifying the agony. I have a real gift for this, he decided.

Jeff followed him, his skull held out in front. "Oooohhh," he wailed, his voice wavering up and down. "Aaaaaaahhhhhh."

Todd was watching Rocky's face behind the window. Her mouth opened wide and he was sure she was yelling for someone to come. When she disappeared from view, they took off.

In seconds they were tearing down the alley behind Rocky's garage. They didn't stop till they were nearly at Alan's house.

"One more time?" Jeff asked, grinning.

"Sure. Maybe Alan'll change his mind about ghosts." Then Todd had a disturbing thought. Alan lived on Maple, and Todd's family lived behind him on Parkview. Only a low fence separated the two backyards.

"It's pretty close to my place," Todd said. "We better be real careful."

"No sweat. I'll wake him up." Jeff couldn't find any gravel, so he heaved wet clods of dirt at Alan's window. Thunk. Thunk. Thunk. Thunk.

"Heavy sleeper," Todd said after a great deal of mud had spattered Alan's window.

"I've got a rock now," Jeff said, hurling it toward the window.

"Not a rock!"

Crash! The window splintered in the night.

"ERROWWWRRR!"

"It's Banshee," Todd whispered horrified. "We set her off and now she'll wake everybody!"

"ERROWWWRRR!"

Alan stuck his head out through the hole in his window. "Who's out there?" he yelled.

"ERROWWWRRR! ERRRROWWWR! ERRR-OWWWRRR!"

Todd glanced toward his house and saw the upstairs lights come on, first in his aunt's room, then his parents'.

"ERROWWWRRR!" Banshee's yowl could, as Todd's father said, nearly wake the dead.

"Let's get out of here!" cried Jeff.

"Is that you, Jeff? Todd, you out there?"

Todd looked over his shoulder and saw Alan, his glasses on, gazing in the direction of Jeff's voice.

Alan's parents were out in the yard now. Todd saw his own father dash down the back steps of their house. "Here, Banshee. Here kitty, kitty, kitty," came his dad's voice.

"Rrooff! Rrooff!" barked Inky.

"Yowp! Yowp! Yowp!" added the beagle next to Alan's house.

Gossamer fabric streaming behind them, Todd and Jeff fled. They made the block and a half in flying time and shinnied up the pillar onto the porch roof, tumbling through the window into Jeff's bedroom just as the phone rang.

"Who'd be . . . calling now?" panted Jeff. "It's . . . after midnight!"

"Get in bed and cover up," Todd said shakily.

The door to Jeff's room opened a crack.

Todd made sleepy breathing sounds under his sheet.

Jeff made no sound whatsoever.

Steps came across the room to the twin beds. "Jeff?" whispered his father. "You'll suffocate under there."

Todd thought his heart might leap out of his chest.

"Jeff? Jeff! What are you —? What's this thing? Good Lord, what have you been up to?"

Todd peeked over the edge of his sheet and saw Mr. Lorimer holding up the skull.

11. One Long Night

Mr. Lorimer sat down on the edge of Jeff's bed. "Let's have it," he said. "I just talked to Todd's dad. It seems there was a real racket over their way, and Alan was calling your name and Todd's. Now I'm just going to sit here until you tell me where you boys have been."

Todd threw off his sheet. "Right," he said, wanting to explain and be done with it. "The idea was to scare Rocky, and it went great! So we tried it at Alan's place —"

"It's all my fault," Jeff inserted.

"Whoa," said Mr. Lorimer. "From the beginning."

Jeff told the story. "And, Dad," he said, "it would have been okay except I threw that rock. . . . Boy, why'd I ever throw a rock, anyway? Was that dumb!"

"Yes, sir, world-class stupid," his father agreed. "But I give you credit for telling the truth."

"If I don't, I get cremated around here."

"I'm just the man to handle that," Mr. Lorimer said dryly. "Anyway, the window isn't the worst of it. The famous Banshee yowl has really upset Todd's aunt. You boys have some tall apologizing to do. And now I have to drive Todd home."

On the way, Todd tried to explain further why they had wanted to "fix" Rocky. "She's been driving us crazy with this ghost stuff," he told Jeff's dad. "Ever since Aunt Morbelia."

Mr. Lorimer pulled up in Todd's driveway and turned off the engine. "I don't claim to understand girls," he said, "because Princess is our first female and she's still a baby, but I remember the girls in sixth grade."

"Rocky hates being a girl!"

Jeff's dad shook his head. "She doesn't have any choice. And she's changing a great deal now, more than you guys. Think about that, okay?" He patted Todd's shoulder and said, "Come on, let's go in and face the music."

Several very unpleasant minutes followed. Todd's folks listened to the tale of the haunting with sober faces. His father was especially worried about Aunt Morbelia.

"Where is she?" Todd asked. "I could say I'm sorry right now. And I'd better find Banshee. She'll yowl again if she feels like it."

"God forbid," said Mr. Fearing. Turning to Jeff's dad he said, "Thanks, Jim. Sorry to mess up your sleep, but Todd won't be spending the night at your place for a while anyway. See you on the first tee. Seven-thirty, right?"

Mr. Lorimer grinned. "That golf game is sounding earlier every minute. If we were younger, we'd just stay up. Don't be too hard on Todd, Bruce. Remember, it was Jeff's idea all along. Good night, now."

"Todd should have known better," his mom said as Jeff's dad went out the door.

"Where's Aunt Morbelia?" Todd asked again.

"In her room and not to be disturbed," his dad replied. "Todd, I just don't see why —"

"Enough, Bruce, please," said Mrs. Fearing. "Can't you see he feels awful? I'm sure neither of the boys had any idea of what could happen. They certainly never set out to terrify Morbelia."

"That's for sure," Todd said. And it had been such a great idea. . . . "Can I go look for Banshee now?" he asked.

"I'll go with you," his dad said. "We have to find her if it takes all night."

"First, give me my fabric samples," said his mother. "If they don't come clean, it will be your responsibility to pay for replacements. They're expensive, you know."

Todd fished the wispy pieces of fabric out of his gym bag and handed them over. "Sorry," he said. "I never thought there'd be mud."

"You didn't think, period," said his father. "Now let's find that blasted cat."

They pulled on jackets and went out into the damp, unfriendly night — the night that had been so perfect before. "Here, kitty, kitty," Todd called repeatedly.

On the second round of their block, his dad grumbled, "Black cat, black night. This is ridiculous."

Still, Todd was as stubborn as his cat, and he knew how she thought. "Maybe she went over to bug that beagle next to Alan's," he suggested. "Let's try over on Maple, Dad."

A few minutes later, Todd saw Banshee crouched against a white garage next to the Harrimans'. "Don't move," Todd warned his father.

Todd sat down on the wet grass and called, "Here, Banshee, good kitty," as calmly as if he were sitting on the porch. She'd run away if she figured out he was after her.

Banshee turned toward Todd. She flicked her ears and tail for several annoyed seconds before she gave in to his wheedling and ambled over. "Merrowwr?"

"Come on." Todd patted his lap. "What a pretty kitty. Come on, up on my lap."

When she came within range, he grabbed her.

"MeeeYOW," she snarled, knowing she'd been tricked.

"Ha-ha, Pussycat," said Mr. Fearing. "You have just spent your last night outdoors."

"Aw, Dad —"

"No arguments. I have gotten up in the night with that animal for the last time. It's embarrassing to have her wake the neighbors, and tonight was a disaster. Your aunt was sure it was the wail of the banshee. Now I know it's crazy, but I'm not putting her through that again."

"But where —"

"In the basement. I'll let her out at six when I get up, and that will have to do."

"But cats are —"

"Night animals. I know. Good cats stay out at night and no one cares. Bad cats belong indoors where they can't bother anyone. We've been letting her make the rules long enough. We give in to her all the time."

He paused, and when he went on his tone was thoughtful. "Just where would you be, Todd, if you caved in like that on other things? What if you said, 'Well, I give up. I can't learn words'? Think about that."

Todd knew how close he had come to giving up — hundreds of times. "Yeah," he said slowly. "You're right. Banshee's spoiled. I guess that's my fault, too."

Mr. Fearing put his arm around Todd's shoulders. "Don't take on the guilt of the world," he said. "We all got a kick out of her being naughty. We'll be stricter from now on and it won't hurt her, you'll see."

At home they put a disgusted cat in the basement and went upstairs. At Todd's door his dad said, "We'll see about replacing the Harrimans' window tomorrow. You and Jeff can share the cost out of your allowances. And please think about an apology to your aunt."

"Sure, Dad. 'Night." Todd dropped his clothes in a heap and crawled into bed, nudging Inky to one side. Inky woke up long enough to wash Todd's face and ear.

"Hi, Ink. Bad-news night." Except he remembered Rocky's face in the window. He was sure they'd scared her. One good thing, anyway. Too bad Alan had heard Jeff's voice. Otherwise, they might have gotten away.

When he woke late Saturday morning, Todd went downstairs to apologize to his aunt.

"She's still in her room," his mother told him, "and I'm worried. However, my fabric samples came clean. It's darn lucky you chose washable materials. I suppose I don't need to tell you never to do anything like that again."

"You don't need to tell me."

"Well, I'm telling you anyway. Now what are we going to do about Aunt Morbelia?"

"Is Dad golfing?"

"Yes. I'm afraid she's our problem."

Todd didn't say anything. He turned around and went back upstairs — marching down the hall to his aunt's room — taking firm, quick steps — knocking loudly on her door before he lost his nerve.

"Aunt Morbelia? It's me, Todd. Can I come in?"

He heard only silence for a few seconds. Then she said, "I am resting this morning, thank you."

"Are you sick?"

"No, Todd, I am not sick."

"Then why're you resting?"

"I am resting because I choose to."

"Do you want some coffee?"

"No, thank you."

"But you always have coffee in the morning."

"Not today, thank you."

"Are you real, real sure?"

More silence. At last she said, "I think you may as well come in, Todd."

Do it fast, he told himself. He yanked open the door and saw her sitting in the tall rocker, a book open in her lap. He had seen her this way before, in her robe, her hair braided in one thick plait.

As before, he sat down on the bed. He wanted her to hear the whole story so she'd understand, and he wasn't going to beat around the bush. He couldn't "work up to it" the way Rocky always did. "I'm sure sorry about last night. We never meant to scare you," he began.

She nodded.

"But we did want to scare Rocky," he continued, "and that went fine — anyway I hope it did. And then, there we were at Alan's house. . . ."

He went on to explain how much fun it would have been to tease Alan, and how Jeff had gotten overexcited and thrown a rock because Alan was such a sound sleeper. He tried to tell everything.

At the end he said, "Banshee's a pain and it's all my fault, but she won't ever wake people up at night again because now she has to stay in the basement."

Todd figured that was about it. He had apologized as thoroughly as he knew how. "So can you come downstairs now?" he asked.

"I . . . I do not understand, Todd, why you wanted to scare Rocky. Can you explain that?"

"Sure. She's been asking for it lately! She used to be a lot of fun. Sometimes it was just her and Alan and Jeff and me, but lots of times we had a big group. And lately, all she cares about . . ." Todd stopped, sadly aware that he had said too much.

"I see," she replied, her eyes on his face. She was quiet then, looking down at her lap. "Just as I feared," she said, more to herself than to him.

Todd started to protest but she held up her hand.

"No. Do not say anything. None of this is your fault, Todd. If I had not come here, Rocky's interest would not have been drawn to me. And you would not have been out there last night trying to cure her of her fascination. The cat would not have disturbed anyone, and —"

Todd had to interrupt. "I'm sorry, Aunt Morbelia, but Banshee's done that lots of times. Anything can set her off. That's not your fault."

She nodded. "Nonetheless, I was foolish to react the way I did. After all, I have heard cats in the night before.

"But I was especially foolish to keep on telling the tales that have always intrigued me — that used to amuse your father and that do so appeal to a child like Rocky. I have done exactly what I wished not to do. I have interfered in your life."

"Not on purpose!" he burst out.

"Of course not."

At last Todd felt he was making progress. He relaxed and began to smile. "Okay," he said, "so now we're even."

She looked him in the eyes, a long, penetrating gaze. He nearly gave way, but he made himself return her look, and at last she smiled too.

"For someone who has trouble with words," she said, "you do extremely well."

Todd hopped off the bed. "Thanks. Can you come downstairs now?"

"Is that important to you?"

"Oh yeah. I'm in a lot of trouble. And Mom's worried with you up here."

"Well, we do not want that," she said briskly, closing the book and standing up. "I shall see what I can do on your behalf. I think that you and Jeff should go fishing today. Something normal and healthy."

For a second, Todd's hopes rose. But he knew his parents. "Thanks," he said, "but I'm grounded and I'll bet Jeff is, too. I'll call him and see how mad his folks are. His mom can be real tough."

Todd left her and went to the upstairs phone. "How's it going at your place?" he asked when Jeff answered.

"Not too swift," Jeff said. "I'm grounded this weekend for sure. Mom said we had to fix the Harrimans' window and apologize to them — and to Rocky. And we have to think of something nice to do for your aunt. You got any ideas?"

"Apologize to Rocky? No way!"

"Maybe we can fake it. How about your aunt?"

"Aunt Morbelia and I got it all worked out. She's not mad."

"My mom is," Jeff said glumly.

"Relax. We'll think of something."

12. The Highlights of Hampshire

Being grounded for the weekend hadn't been a tragedy, Todd decided Sunday evening. He had seen lots of funny TV programs, including an hour of Disney cartoons, his favorites. He had bathed Inky, brushed Banshee, and caught up on his homework for Miss King. When he left for school Monday morning, he was in a cheerful mood.

Rocky was anything but cheery. "I hear you guys are in a lot of trouble," she said in the hall outside their class. "Serves you right. Anyway, I knew who it was right off." She made a face at him and stomped into the classroom.

Oh yeah? Then why are you so mad? Todd thought. I bet we scared her purple and she's covering up.

As soon as Jeff arrived, Todd repeated what Rocky had said. "So I think we did it, don't you?" he asked Jeff.

"If she's real ticked off, we did it. Probably worth the cost of that dumb window. Mom says I have to pay for it because I threw the rock."

As they went toward their seats, Todd said, "No, that's not fair. I'm paying half."

The homeroom teacher called for order and Todd didn't have a chance to talk to Alan until recess.

At recess, Alan told Todd and Jeff, "I'm real sorry, you guys." Through his thick lenses, Alan's eyes looked almost teary. "I tried to explain when you came Saturday about the window, but my dad was always in the way. I didn't mean to get you in trouble! See, I knew it was Banshee, and I thought I heard Jeff's voice and —"

"It's okay," Todd said. "Everybody's cooling off."

"We're going to do something nice for Todd's aunt," added Jeff. "Then we can forget it. We fixed Rocky and that's what counts."

Alan gestured to the far corner of the playground. "See that? She's with a bunch of *girls.*"

"You're kidding!" Todd looked where Alan had pointed. There she was, with three other girls, sitting under a tree and talking. He remembered what Jeff's dad had said in the car, echoing what he had noticed earlier. Rocky was changing, all right.

"She's never done that before!" Jeff said. "What's the matter with her?"

"She's a girl," said Todd.

"Hunh!" Jeff snorted. "So forget *her.* Come on. Let's make up teams for soccer."

Jeff kept Todd company on the way to the learning center that afternoon. Both were trying to think of some way to apologize to Aunt Morbelia . . . and satisfy Jeff's mother.

"A big candy bar?" Jeff suggested. "Or flowers?"

"Maybe, but I bet she got that stuff all the time when she was a teacher." Todd remembered how thrilled his aunt had been when he handed her the books from Miss King. "She likes books," he said.

"A cookbook!"

"Nah, she'd think we want her to cook something for us. It's kind of like asking."

They stopped at the corner while a Greyhound bus moseyed through the intersection. "Dumb tourists," Jeff said, glaring at a lady who stared at them through the window. "I hate it when they're in town."

"That's it!" yelled Todd. "We'll take her to all the old houses — the ones with those little signs. And the caves, maybe. . . . Mom's been trying to take her on one of those tours for weeks."

"We'd be better guides — much better," Jeff said. "And our funeral home's got a plaque, you know — 1791 in brass letters. It's real impressive."

"Yup. We can do it tomorrow. And let's make it a surprise." Todd hopped up the steps to the learning center. "Bye. See you after dinner.

He slipped into his seat just as Miss King began writing on the board. She turned and gave him a pretend frown. "You're all alone, darn it. We convinced your aunt to come and observe, but we haven't seen her yet. Please nag her gently, just for me."

Todd promised and Miss King went back to writing

on the board. He looked out the window at another blue sky. Always on learning-center days. Barfaroma.

He remembered what Rocky had said about a movie called *The Exorcist*. The girl in it was supposed to be possessed by the devil. She had thrown up this yukky-colored vomit all over the place. That was just how he felt now. Puke on the learning center. At least in the summer his class began at 8:30 and ended at 11:00. And someday . . . maybe . . .

"Yoo-hoo? Todd?" Miss King called. "Come to the party."

After school on Wednesday, Todd and Jeff jogged home to take Aunt Morbelia on a tour of historic Hampshire, Ohio. Because of its small-town atmosphere and beautiful, old homes, Hampshire drew many tourists, especially in the spring and fall. Everyone's favorite stop was the old-fashioned ice-cream parlor on Center Street. The boys planned to end their tour at the soda fountain there.

"She's going to flip over this," Jeff whispered as they reached the door at Todd's house. In the kitchen, they found Aunt Morbelia writing a letter.

"Hi," Todd said. "Can you come for a little walk?"

"With you boys?"

"Yes, ma'am," Jeff answered. "Right now, okay?"

Aunt Morbelia folded her hands in her lap. "May I ask why, and where we are going?"

Todd said, "We can't tell you. It's a secret."

"A surprise," Jeff added. "You'll like it."

"I do like surprises." She stood up. "I shall leave a note for your mother, Todd, explaining that we are out."

When they were outside, Todd suggested they go east on Parkview first, to the caves. They set off down the street, Aunt Morbelia towering between them, her black skirts a strange contrast to their bare legs and shorts.

"The Hampshire caves are very famous," Jeff began in the singsong tone of a professional guide. "For centuries these caves have been hideouts. Before the Civil War, slaves hid in them on the way north.

"You can get lost in there," he went on. "Once on a Scout campout, that drippy kid from Chillicothe — Carl, I think — was gone for hours."

"I see," said Aunt Morbelia, who sounded as if she didn't see at all. "Perhaps just looking in will be sufficient."

The caves were admired briefly as she had suggested. They trooped back on Parkview past Todd's house and west toward the town park and lake.

"This's our favorite place," Todd explained as they stood on the end of the dock. "We catch real nice fish here. Sometimes we rent rowboats and go all over. It isn't very deep, so nobody worries much."

"You have to wear a life jacket," Jeff added. "See the white raft way out there? Pretty soon it'll be warm enough to swim, and if you've passed the test, you can go out to the raft. That's a blast."

"See the pretty trees all around the lake?" Todd waited till his aunt took notice. "The Lion's Club put those out a long time ago, when I was a baby. It was Dad's idea. When it's real hot, this's the coolest place in town."

They walked back down the dock. "See the new roof on the boat shack?" Jeff asked, pointing upward as they passed the small wooden building. "Our funeral home donated that just last fall. It was leaking like crazy before."

"Very nice," said Aunt Morbelia. "I think I am beginning to get the idea. We are on a tour of your favorite places, is that correct?"

"Close," Todd said. "We're going to see all the famous places in Hampshire. It's a historic district, you know."

"Yes, your mother has been itching to get me on a tour. Now I am glad I waited. Somehow, I feel that this will be a more interesting experience."

Todd and Jeff looked proudly at one another. "Let's do the homes now," Todd said.

They began with Donner House, the oldest brick home in Hampshire. Although she wasn't open at the time, the lady who lived in Donner House was so proud of it she agreed to take them around. They were expected to admire the beechwood stair railings and newel posts, the wide oak floorboards, each original pane of glass.

"This's taking forever," Jeff muttered.

Todd whispered, "Maybe we won't see all the houses. Your place is kind of depressing. We could skip it."

"No way! Ours is the third-oldest in the whole town!"

When they finally escaped the Donner House hostess, they continued down Center Street to Morrison House, a small, yellow-frame building owned by the middle-school principal. His wife knew Todd and Jeff, and was delighted to meet Aunt Morbelia, whom she had heard about.

She began a well-rehearsed talk, dwelling on the herbs, bulbs, and trees in their backyard. "Absolutely faithful to the original plan of the gardens," she announced.

"Yawwwn," groaned Todd when the women were several feet away. "Why do they have to tell everything?"

"Beats me," Jeff said. "I'm sure sorry I threw that rock. Good thing my place is next. Aunt Morbelia's pretty old. This's enough for one day."

"Yeah. Then we can get ice cream."

At last Aunt Morbelia said they must be going. Jeff led the way to his house and the rambling, attached building that was Lorimer's Funeral Home.

"You saw my house at Mom's coffee party," Jeff said. "It isn't very old, just the living room and my folks' room over it, but here's the really good part. See? Seventeen hundred ninety-one, right on the plaque."

Jeff turned the huge brass knob in the center of the oaken door. "Dad said he'd be here. Come on."

Aunt Morbelia stood erect and still, her eyes on the

newer brass plaque — the one that read "Lorimer's Funeral Parlor."

Todd looked up at her face and knew they were making a mistake. "I don't think —" he began.

"Hurry up!" called Jeff, now inside the foyer.

"Are you all right?" Todd asked his aunt. "Maybe we should go home."

Aunt Morbelia's chin rose. "I shall be fine. I can see how proud Jeff is of this old building. He would be hurt if we did not at least step in a moment and admire it." Resolutely, she went ahead of him through the doorway.

The orchestral music, delicate and flutelike, seemed a natural part of the elegant interior. The air smelled only faintly of flowers. Good, Todd thought, praying that the viewing rooms were empty. Even one nice fresh corpse might be too many.

Todd said, "I still think we ought to —"

"Good afternoon, Madam," came the oily voice of Mr. Johnson, the assistant director. Todd and Jeff hated him and his gray hair, gray suits, and gray skin. His pointy nose twitched as he peered at them through small, round glasses. In private, Todd and Jeff called him The Mole.

Jeff's dad wasn't happy with Mr. Johnson's manner either, but he was an expert at makeup, and Lorimer's was known for its good-looking corpses.

"Where's Dad?" Jeff asked. "He's supposed to be here."

"What a pity," soothed Mr. Johnson, groping for

Aunt Morbelia's hand. "He's been called to the home of one newly deceased." He captured the hand he sought and imprisoned it against his suit lapel.

"Be assured, Madam, that I can assist you in the absence of Mr. Lorimer, and will be only too happy to do so."

Todd wanted to kick The Mole in the shins. "We're fine, thanks," he said loudly. "We just want to show my aunt some of the old stuff in here and then we're going. It's a historic tour, that's all. Bye."

Aunt Morbelia, who had appeared rather undone, now snatched her hand away from Mr. Johnson. "We do not require any assistance," she said. "Please go about your business."

"Yeah," Jeff added rudely. "Come on, you guys, we can look at the casket room. It's the oldest."

Aunt Morbelia, back straight, followed Jeff. Todd had no choice but to go along. One room, he told himself, and we're getting out of here. I don't care how old this place is, this's a dumb idea.

"Oh, my," Aunt Morbelia gasped as they stepped into the casket room.

"It's great, isn't it?" Jeff said, glowing. "These are all original wood moldings, and the ceiling's been kept the same, too. See those little white angels and harps and flowers? Those are plaster molds, all made by hand. Dad says they haven't made ceilings like this in a hundred years.

"And over here, behind this thing" — Jeff stopped talking long enough to roll a casket away from the

wall — "is a wall safe, only nobody could ever tell! Now watch." He pressed one edge of the molding and an entire wood panel swung out to reveal a metal safe set in the wall.

"Oh, my," Aunt Morbelia said again, more a whimper than words.

Todd watched her eyes, looking not at the cleverly hidden safe or the antique wood moldings or the cherubs on the ceiling, but at the caskets themselves. It was, after all, a room filled with boxes for the dead.

"We're going home," he said firmly. If Jeff got ticked off, tough beanos. He didn't like the way his aunt was acting. Her face had sort of crumpled and she seemed unsteady. "Come on," he said, reaching for her hand.

Aunt Morbelia let Todd lead her from the casket room.

"Geez!" Jeff said, following behind. "Dad isn't even back yet. And don't go out the front! She's seen that part. Come back through the side hall like all the tours."

Aunt Morbelia followed where Todd took her. He was almost yanking her down the hallway in his eagerness to get outdoors.

"These are the original wall murals for the first Lorimer Funeral Home," Jeff was saying. Just then the door to the outside swung open. One man held the door back while another wheeled a stretcher inside. On the stretcher lay a body covered with a white sheet. Mr. Lorimer followed the stretcher.

"Dad!" Jeff called. "We're here, just like I said."

Todd pulled his aunt over against the wall to make room for the stretcher. As it went past, a naked leg flopped free and dangled over the side.

Mr. Lorimer caught Aunt Morbelia just as she toppled forward.

13. Aunt Morbelia's Decision

Mr. Lorimer lowered Aunt Morbelia gently to the floor. He called for smelling salts and Mr. Johnson came running, holding the bottle out in front of him and murmuring, "Oh dear, what a calamity."

Todd and Jeff stood nearby, stiff against the wall. Todd wondered if they had killed his aunt. In the funeral home.

He pressed his lips together, afraid he would cry. That would be awful. Boys of eleven didn't cry in public — not if they could help it. But Mr. Johnson was right for once. This was a calamity.

Unable to speak, he stared at his aunt's face. When her eyelids fluttered and she moved her head, he knew she wasn't dead. He sagged downward until he was sitting on the floor, his head on his knees. Jeff slid down beside him.

"She's okay. Look," Jeff whispered.

Todd raised his head just as his aunt was struggling to sit up. "I have never . . . never done that," she said weakly.

"Don't try to sit up yet," Mr. Lorimer told her. "Just rest your head on my arm a few minutes. Then I'll drive you and Todd home."

He turned to eye Todd and Jeff. "Can you explain how you came to be here?" he asked, voice cold.

"But, Dad, I said —"

"You said you were bringing her to our place. I assumed you meant the house."

"But it's a historic tour," Jeff explained. "Like a *real* tour, with the wood moldings and the safe, and —"

Normally a pink, amiable man, Jeff's dad was now red with fury. "How could you *possibly* —"

"Mr. Lorimer," Aunt Morbelia interrupted, "you must not blame your son. I asked the boys to take me on this tour. They were merely obliging me."

Todd and Jeff shared their thoughts without speaking. Then Jeff whispered, "Now what do we say?"

Mr. Lorimer took over, and neither of them had a chance to say anything. He helped Aunt Morbelia to her feet and, with aid from Mr. Johnson, seated her in the Lorimers' family car. "Bob, call Doc Campbell and tell him to hotfoot it over to Bruce Fearing's place.

"You boys get in the backseat," he ordered.

On the way to Todd's house, Aunt Morbelia said, "I feel no need of a physician. If I had had any notion that I was going to faint, I could have prevented it. However, it happened rather suddenly and I was not prepared."

"I believe that's the way it usually happens," said Jeff's dad, smiling. He was still pinker than normal, but Todd was relieved to see him smile.

"Nonetheless," Mr. Lorimer continued, "I'll feel better and so will you when Doc Campbell has had a look-see. He's a fine doctor, a real institution here in Hampshire."

In his driveway, Todd leapt out of the car and opened the door for his aunt. Mr. Lorimer bustled around the front of the car, saying, "I'll get her."

"Todd's arm will be sufficient, thank you," said Aunt Morbelia. "I really am quite recovered."

But she isn't, Todd thought, feeling how she depended on him to steady her. She's lying again so we won't get in trouble.

Mrs. Fearing came flying out to the porch. "What happened? Where have you been? Aunt Morbelia, how —"

"I am fine, Sunny," soothed Aunt Morbelia. "I have been on an historic tour of the town, thanks to the boys, but an unfortunate incident caused me to faint. Mr. Lorimer has called the doctor and there is nothing to worry about."

As soon as Aunt Morbelia was in her room, Mr. Lorimer phoned his office. Todd's dad came home as he was hanging up the telephone. "The message went through and Doc Campbell's on his way," he told Mrs. Fearing.

To Mr. Fearing he said, "Your aunt has had a fainting spell, I'm sorry to say, in my funeral home. Todd will tell you all about it. I have to get back to work, but I'll be phoning this evening to check on her."

He left and Todd sank into the living-room couch. His parents were going to demand an explanation. Jeff's parents would, too, and their stories had better be alike. In fact, they'd better be what Aunt Morbelia had said, even if it wasn't the truth.

"Todd," called Aunt Morbelia. "Come up here, please."

"We'll be waiting when you get back downstairs," his dad said. "And make it snappy."

"Now, Bruce, you don't know anything about this yet, and neither do I," said Mrs. Fearing.

Todd fled to his great-aunt's room. He knocked once to warn her he was coming in. She was already in bed, covered up to her chin even though it was hot. Today, she looked at least seventy-four.

He stood beside her and started to speak, but she held up her hand. "Do not say anything. I understand. You were right and we should never have gone inside. I should have listened to you. Now, I want you to listen to me."

At that point Inky padded into the bedroom. He hadn't been in this room for a long time. When he saw Todd and Aunt Morbelia, his two favorite people, he bounded to the side of the bed and put his nose next to Aunt Morbelia's hand.

"Inky, get away," Todd said.

Inky didn't budge. He whined and nudged Aunt Morbelia's hand until she lifted it and placed it on his head. Then he closed his eyes and stood still.

Todd's aunt tapped the dog's head softly with her fingers. "Todd," she said, "you and Jeff had made a lovely plan to entertain me. The reason behind it is not important. You could never have imagined what would happen, and I will not hear of your being punished for it. Is that clear?"

"We were going to the ice-cream parlor next," he said. "All the tours do that as the last stop."

She nodded. "Just as I said, a lovely plan. But I was right back in April. I do not fit into your lives here. I am going to leave, Todd, and I wanted you to know first, so that you would not think it was your fault."

"But you —"

"No arguments, please. I have been considering this from the start. You know that. And much as I love you and your parents, this has been a difficult adjustment for me. I am probably too old to change. Even so, it has been a wonderful experience knowing you. You have taught me a great deal, Todd, and I am grateful."

"Miss Fearing?" Dr. Campbell poked his head in the door. "Hello, Todd. If you'll just excuse us for a moment," he said, coming in and setting his bag on the chair.

"No!" Todd cried. "I have to —"

"Not now, Todd," commanded his aunt.

Todd turned and left the room. Inky stayed in place as Dr. Campbell introduced himself to Aunt Morbelia.

Walking down the steps, Todd had never felt so helpless. She was going to leave, and no matter what she said, it was his fault. He was the reason she couldn't fit in here. He and his friends and Banshee.

He hadn't wanted her to come. She knew that. Did she still believe he didn't want her? When she had said she was leaving, his first thought had been NO! And then, how will I ever learn all the months in order? How can I go back to doing homework alone — and not as well?

She was right about not fitting in, though. She didn't slip into place like a piece in a jigsaw puzzle. Nothing about her was small or simple or insignificant. Instead of fitting in, she made her own place. That's how she was and he understood it now.

Todd stumbled on the last step, righted himself, and went over to the sofa. Immediately his mother sat beside him. "What is it, honey? What's the matter?"

That did it. Tears burned in his eyes and flowed down his cheeks and he couldn't stop them, much as he tried. Without meaning to, he had messed everything up. Where would she go? To an old-folks' home? He knew now just how wrong that would be.

Through his tears he said, "She's leaving."

Banshee crawled out from under the sofa, gave one look at Todd and his mother, and streaked up the stairway to the second floor.

Before Dr. Campbell came back downstairs, Todd had managed to stop crying. He explained how the idea of a town tour had backfired and why Aunt Morbelia had fainted.

"Good Lord," said Mr. Fearing. "Who'd think they'd come in with a dead body when you were there? The odds against that have to be a million to one."

"I tried not to go in at all," Todd repeated. "I really did, and she said she wanted to."

His parents nodded together, their faces grave.

"How are we going to keep her from leaving?" asked Todd's mother. "I've grown terribly fond of her. She's always so happy when we're visiting together or cooking in the kitchen. I thought it was working out."

"Me, too," Todd said, hiccuping. He hated crying. It made him feel like a baby and he always hiccuped afterward. Still, he was thinking more clearly now. Why is Aunt Morbelia giving up so soon? he wondered. She sure wouldn't let *me* do that.

Dr. Campbell descended the steps, swinging his bag. "You folks can put away those long faces," he said. "I think she'll be fine after a day's rest. You can run some tea or soup up to her from time to time, but she has two noble guardians, so I expect her to rest well."

"Two noble guardians?" demanded Todd's father.

"The dog and the cat. The dog has his head on the bed and the cat's in the chair. I asked if I should shoo them out and she said, 'No. They are even more stubborn than I am. Let them be.' So I did."

Hope took root in Todd's mind as he listened to what Dr. Campbell was saying. She doesn't really want to go, he decided. She'd never let Inky and Banshee stay otherwise. Especially Banshee.

Okay, he thought, it's time to fight. Just like Miss King said. You get good and mad and you fight back.

He jumped up from the couch. "I have to make a bunch of phone calls," he said.

14. A Good Fight

By the time Todd and his mother settled down to read at bedtime, Todd's plan to change his aunt's mind was in place. Now he could only wait.

"Did you say good night to Aunt Morbelia?" his mom asked.

"Yup. Banshee went back up there after she ate, you know. Inky's on that furry little rug by her bed."

"Good. Animals can be a tremendous comfort," she said, opening the book. "Anyway, we're not letting her go without a fight. We can be stubborn, too."

Todd was amused. This whole family's incredibly stubborn, he thought.

"'Rikki-Tikki-Tavi' by Rudyard Kipling," his mother began. "'This is the story of the great war that Rikki-tikki-tavi fought single-handed, through the bath-rooms of the big bungalow in Segowlee cantonment. Darzee, the tailor-bird, helped him, and Chuchun-dra, the musk-rat, who never comes out in the middle of the floor, but always creeps round by the wall, gave him advice; but Rikki-tikki did the real fighting.'"

Todd let himself be caught up in the story. It was an old favorite and, like Inky, very comforting.

Todd got up at six the next morning and did his homework alone. It seemed to take longer alone. At breakfast, his father was silent. At last he said, "We can't order her to stay."

"I know," Todd replied. "I've got an idea —"

"No more ideas."

"Dad? Trust me, please?"

His father looked at Todd's set face and slowly he nodded. "I'm sorry. I know you're upset. We all are. But this may be your last chance, so be careful."

All Thursday, until three, when the bell rang, Todd forced himself to pay attention, to listen, to do his work.

After school he and Jeff left a note in the learning center's office to explain why Todd would be absent that day. Then they went to the flower shop. "We need something pretty for an old lady," Todd told the clerk, "but we don't have much money."

They left the shop with four white carnations and a red rose. "What if there's something unlucky about carnations?" Jeff asked. "We know roses can cause shipwrecks."

"The rose is the badge of England, remember? And white's got to be a good color. You just can't think about dumb old superstitions all the time. It's crazy."

Todd grew quiet, concentrating on the job ahead.

He was the cleanup batter, after all. He had sent others ahead of him, but he had to score, too.

"Say your stuff very carefully," he reminded Jeff. "She has to think this's all your idea."

When they got to Aunt Morbelia's room, Todd went in first. Inky raised his head off the floor to be petted, but he didn't leave his place by the bed. Banshee glared at him because he was disturbing her afternoon nap, until slowly her eyelids closed and her head swayed in sleep.

Aunt Morbelia lay still, eyes shut, but she was not asleep. One long, slender hand was rhythmically tapping the bed beside her.

She looks funny, he thought. Her eyes are red and sort of puffy. I think she's been crying. What could have gone wrong? What could possibly have happened this time?

Gently he said, "Jeff's brought you something."

Her eyes flew open. "Like everyone else?" she asked, gesturing around the room.

Only then did he see the flowers. On the windowsill, a blooming plant. On the dresser, two vases full of cut flowers. On her bedside table, a small cactus garden with a yellow sash round its terra-cotta bowl.

Jeff stepped into the room and saw the floral display immediately. "Well, poop," he said. "I thought I had such a cool idea. This looks just like my dad's funer —"

"Jeff!" yelled Todd.

A quiet laugh intervened. It wasn't Jeff. It couldn't be Inky or Banshee. It had to be Aunt Morbelia.

"You're laughing!" Todd said.

"Yes, yes, I am. I have done a fair amount of that today — and some crying, between visitors. Come over here, Jeff, so that I may admire your flowers."

She took them from him and raised the small bouquet to her nose. "A red rose. My favorite. And carnations have such a lovely fragrance. You did not have to do this, of course, but I thank you."

Jeff smiled and Todd gave him a hard look. He wanted him to say his piece and go. One mistake was plenty.

"I'm glad you like them," Jeff said, his voice formal. "I felt really bad about what happened on our tour yesterday. I should have remembered about your sister . . . your sister . . ."

"Dying," inserted Aunt Morbelia. "It is all right, Jeff. You were only hoping to show me beautiful things. I know that. No apology is necessary."

"Oh yes it is," Jeff said earnestly. "My folks are about to give up on me. Dad said they were raising a juvenile delinquent and maybe I should go away to military school."

"Codswallop," said Aunt Morbelia. "I can tell your father about some real juvenile delinquents, boys I knew long ago. You have not got the first notion of how to be a bad boy, not really. I shall call your father this evening and make everything right." She held out

her hand and they shook hands, Jeff looking both em-
barrassed and relieved.

"See you later," Todd said as Jeff left.

And now, he thought, now it's my turn. And I don't
dare goof it up. Not even for a second.

"Todd?"

"Yes?"

"You do not have to say all the things you are standing there preparing to say."

"Yes I do. Otherwise you'll go away and you won't
ever know. And it's important." He held himself tall
and straight beside her bed.

"I know that. You would not have sent all those
people if it were not important. That was the most
touching thing anyone has ever done for me. I cried
many happy tears today."

"They *wanted* to come," he said, glad to hear that
her tears had been happy. "And they weren't supposed to tell. They promised they wouldn't."

"I asked for the truth. The head librarian is a particularly poor liar and she broke down right away."

Todd grinned. He couldn't help himself.

"After that," she went on, "it was easy. Mrs. Lorimer is no longer mad at her son, by the way. Jeff will
find that out when he gets home. His mother gave
me the potted tulips. Your Mr. Darnell brought one
vase of flowers, the librarian, the other. The cactus
garden came from Miss King, of course. She was the
most eloquent of the group.

"And now," she went on, "I am promised round the town. I may have to start getting up at four instead of five."

Todd sank down on the bed. "Good," he said simply. "That's real good. I thought I'd messed everything up."

"Of course not. I am a foolish old woman who hasn't the brains God gave a goose sometimes. But I shall tell you part of our problem. You have been far too polite with me. For instance, if you do not wish to hear a ghost story, say so."

"But everybody else . . ." he began. Then he started over. "I like comedies and cartoons. And animal stories."

"I know that now. Your politeness also allowed Rocky to have her way all the time. You were being the good host. But that led to problems as well, and now we must explain to Rocky. She shall come as my guest for a special treat.

"Todd, you have been so careful of everyone's feelings that we were not aware of *yours*." She paused before going on. "Also, I was missing teaching and here you were, someone to teach. I must have been rather overwhelming. Now, I shall be working at the learning center. I can get it all out of my system there." She smiled and patted Todd's hand.

"Not all!" he burst out, thinking of the last three months he still had to learn, of the new and better homework sessions since her arrival.

She was quiet a moment. Then she said, "Thank

you. And from now on, we shall be very open and honest with one another. Agreed?"

"It's a deal," he said. "Except you have to say, 'It is fun living in Hampshire.'"

"It is fun living in Hampshire."

"Louder."

"It is fun living in Hampshire!"

"Yell."

"IT IS FUN LIVING IN HAMPSHIRE!"

"Excellent," he said. "I believe you now."

"Rrooof! Rrooof!" added Inky, standing up beside the bed. He shoved his muzzle right into Aunt Morbelia's face.

"MeeYOW!" scolded Banshee, leaping down from her chair. She flicked her ears and tail at the two humans and stalked from the room.

Aunt Morbelia sat up. "Get away, Inky. I am capable of washing my own face, thank you. And I cannot stay in this bed one more minute. It is wearing me out.

"Please go downstairs, Todd, and tell your mother I shall be at the table for dinner. I need real food if I am to spend the night sewing . . . and I see that I must."

"Why?"

"I must shorten my skirts. Inky sits on them constantly and he has managed to teach Banshee the same trick. Also, I am afraid your mother is right about all this black. I am to help with the younger children at the learning center this summer, and I do not wish to frighten them. Run on now, Todd, so that I may get dressed."

Todd jumped down the steps, landing in the first-floor hall as his mother came in the door, her arms loaded with groceries. "How's it going?" she asked with a nod at the upstairs.

"Super!" Todd replied. "She's shortening her skirts."